C000090943

The Cat's Graveyard
(+ THE LAST CAST OF THE FLY)

– ANDREW MOAT –

Printed and bound in England by www.printondemand-worldwide.com

http://www.fast-print.net/bookshop

THA CAT'S GRAVEYARD
(+ THE LAST CAST OF THE FLY)
Copyright © Andrew Moat 2016

All rights reserved

No part of this book may be reproduced in any form by photocopying
or any electronic or mechanical means, including information storage
or retrieval systems, without permission in writing from both the
copyright owner and the publisher of the book.

All characters are fictional.
Any similarity to any actual person is purely coincidental.

The right of Andrew Moat to be identified as the author of this work has
been asserted by him in accordance with the Copyright, Designs and
Patents Act 1988 and any subsequent amendments thereto.

A catalogue record for this book is available from the British Library

ISBN 978-178456-440-7

First published 2016 by
FASTPRINT PUBLISHING
Peterborough, England.

The Cat's Graveyard

C ats will, when it appeals to them, bring you gifts. Dead gifts.

It's in their nature. Felines will bring the people closest to them, the ones they share their home with, tokens.

Tokens of their affection. Proof of their prowess and ability to hunt!

It's part and parcel, and if you're lucky enough to share your home with this age-old hunter, then the chances are you will have at some point. Had placed at your feet, or maybe left in some secret place for you to find. The torn and twisted figure that was once a living breathing creature.

Rat, mouse, mole or even rabbit. Its life taken in a swift swipe of a paw or bone-crushing bite from the cat's jaws!

Slices of the dead, left just for you!

I suppose you might, on such discoveries, feel bubble up within your stomach, repulsion and disgust, perhaps even shame, shame that an animal that you care for and hold close to you, like a member of your own family, could feel the need to kill, knowing all the time it's a gift meant to please and impress you.

Yet, after the expected feelings have passed you by, after the shovel finds its place back amongst the rest of the dust-covered tools, in the crowded and clattered shed. After the ritual we seem determined to bequeath upon all living things that die about us.

After it's buried!

You might feel something a little different flutter up inside.

The feeling of flattery!

Standing there, brushing the dirt from your hands, the sun-stroked window, a barrier of glass transparency between you and the cat. Who, looking back at you with half-closed eyes, unquestioned in its loyalty, is proud of its latest token of love.

You might just discover that feeling of flattery flapping its wings. Its presence not quite so strong as shock or disgust. But it's still there all the same. Not unlike a friend fallen on hard times, you offer your help as all good friends do. Yet in the background like a cream-filled tart sat on a table surrounded by savoury sugar-free ones, that feeling of satisfaction.

You ignore it. But it's there all the same!

This was how Richard Cooper felt one summer's day. He stood leaning with one arm against the conservatory's window, the sun baking down through the immaculately clean glass onto his chiselled face. The sunshine felt uplifting. His free hand stuffed into the back pocket of his jeans.

The feeling of flattery and disgust enjoyed a tug-o'-war in his chest.

The Cat was sat in its favourite spot: the lead shingle roof of his shed.

It was a large male. Licking his paw in the morning sunshine, cleaning the remaining blood from its claws, sharp as razors. Richard had gotten the *The Cat* five weeks earlier. His old cat, a gentle and small female called Milly had died in the spring time. The thought had occurred to him not to replace her; she had been Natasha's cat in any case. Not his.

But no matter how hard he had tried to fool himself, he had missed her. After he had buried her small body delicately at the bottom of the garden, he planted a yellow shrub rose over the grave. The only flower in the otherwise-flowerless garden, its main feature the lawn that stretched from fence to fence, one expanse of thick green like a new carpet!

He had missed her so much that the idea of passing through the oncoming winter alone, had rather forced his hand. Finding himself at a re-homing centre for cats, a rather clean and odour-free affair which had pleasantly surprised him, Richard had spotted the large, white, male cat almost at once, picking him out from all the other hopeful candidates.

As the sun beat down on his face, the glass of the conservatory acting like a greenhouse bringing beads of sweat to his forehead, Richard scratched his chin; his stubble had a satisfying rough touch. His mind searched back to the day when he had known without any doubt, that it had to be *The Cat* for him.

The Cat had been sat alone, away from any other of his kind. It had, what had seemed to Richard, an imposing stature. More muscular than any other cat he had ever laid eyes upon. Its fur was whiter than the crispest paper, eyes greener than emeralds that never blinked. Even now after all the time he had spent with *The Cat* he had never once seen *The Cat* blink. The white fur was short about his strong body, accept about the neck and chest, where it grew long and straight. There grew long tufts of white on top of the ears, which were a deep blood-red on the inside.

Rick - Dr Richard Cooper preferred to be called Rick – had enquired about *The Cat's* history, asking the pretty girl that had been showing him around,

"Who's that guy, there, sat by himself?"

"Oh yes, Aslan.

She had giggled like a schoolgirl, her cheeks blushing under the smile of the doctor.

"That's not his name, you know. No, not at all, like. But me and some of the girls we came up with it for him, on account of the fur around his neck, like!"

Rick broadened the smile even more; he hoped he had been successful in hiding his disdain.

There ain't no way I'm taking a cat called 'Aslan' into my house; Natasha would have had a fit!!

The pretty redhead seemed to detect a flicker of his deception, possibly in his eyes; Rick had never been a good poker player.

"But, like, you know, that's not his official name you know, if he suits you and Mary; Mary, that's the boss, she says 'yes' or 'no', like, well, you can decide to call him whatever you like."

Gee, that's just great little miss, let's just hope that big Mary don't hold out no reservations against the doctor. Smile's on overload!!

After a little more digging, and being told, under trim, red eyebrows of flirtation that he was not supposed to be told any of the juicy gossip.

Don't worry little miss, you can trust me, I'm a doctor. No worries, I will keep it our little secret. Big bad Mary won't hear from me. Scouts honour!

The smile had been a winner alright.

The redhead had been cute and about as helpful as she could be. Rick had felt a little sympathy for her, stuck there, in the run-down shelter, cleaning cat trays and sick form the grates.

She had looked around to see if anyone had been listening. Whatever it was she was about to say was real hush-hush!

"Well, Mr Gardener, that's the cat man, well that's what me and some of the girls call him anyway..."

There had been that cheek-reddening giggle again.

"He is the man that brings the strays in, he brings them three, sometimes four, at a time, usually there is a lot of noise, you know the cats been screaming an' all. But this time he had just him like, just Aslan all on his own. He didn't make a single noise, not even when Mary gave him his shots. Me and the girls asked Mr Gardener; he said that the police had called him in, that happens you know, when a cat's owner is dead like. Well, he said that this Aslan was found under the feet of his dead owner!"

She had stopped then, eyes all wide with anticipation for what the handsome doctor might say to this macabre news.

I hope he's neutered, can't have the king of Narnia arching his back up all the wooden chair legs in the house!

Seeing that the news was not going to create any reaction, the girl had carried on, rushing her words like they were bottled up and she couldn't breathe.

"Mr Gardener says that the police had to drag old Aslan away, said he was too fierce, said they had to sedate him like. Cus he kept biting 'em like. He was guarding the body of the old man who had been his owner!"

Yeah, ok love, the cat was fighting for the body of his poor dead owner, true Aslan style!

After that he had met with the white cat who, it seemed to Rick couldn't hurt a fly, let alone fight off a group of people trying to catch him.

He had been neutered before he had arrived with them. The girl had guessed his age to be about seven or eight years, but as there was no past records they couldn't be sure. He had responded well to meeting Rick, and after a rather cold and drawn-out interview with big Mary, who had rather reminded Rick of one of the older sisters on his old ward, he had left with *The Cat* in a carrier under his arm.

The memory was still strong. Even after all those weeks, he remembered how much calmer he had felt. The feeling of loneliness held at bay.

Rick stood now, hands on his hips looking out at *The Cat* on his shed roof. He knew that the sweat on his forehead was not entirely due to the heat of the August morning.

The Cat sat up on its haunches, tilting its head to one side, tail flicking behind its head, green eyes staring, never blinking, staring out at him from across the lawn.

Rick stared back. And scratched his chin.

★ ★ ★

The gifts hadn't started straight away. Like all of *The Cat's* species, it had taken time for it to accept his new surroundings.

Rick had watched it, as it snaked about the living room and conservatory of his bungalow. It had moved about with the air of someone who didn't quite seem at their own social level. As though the bungalow was beneath its standing.

Rick had often wondered where it had come from, and had always thought of the previous owner as being an old colonel. Richer than rich. Marble staircase perhaps, acres of territory for it to roam in, catching mice and rats. Ten bedrooms of which it had the run of all, a kitchen full of beds and diced trout every night!

The Cat was certainly different from any other cat he had ever owned!

After a time, a few days at least, *The Cat* had settled down easily enough. Within two weeks it was well and truly master of the house, always leading Rick when leaving or entering a room, or demanding to be fed first, something Rick pretended not to like, but secretly found very amusing.

By three weeks *The Cat* couldn't be without him. Mewing loudly whenever he left the house. Crying earnestly at his return. Incessant rubbing on his legs and shins whilst he sat in the conservatory, Rick's favourite room, or out on the patio. It would seem to capture Rick with those deep green eyes that sparkled day and night. Rick felt that those eyes held deep within them hidden dark secrets; they would latch onto him wherever he went. When he was occupied by some household job he would suddenly feel the hairs rise on the back of his neck, turning to find *The Cat* looking at him.

Never blinking!

It had turned its nose up bashfully, to any basket or bed Rick had brought home for it to sleep in, insisting with loud cries and blood-curdling moans that it was to sleep on the foot of his bed. Something that he would never have allowed Milly to have done. Very often Rick would awaken, blurry-eyed and dry-mouthed to find its green emeralds staring inches from his face, its breath gently tapping his face.

By the fourth week since getting *The Cat* home, Rick decided to let it out into the garden. Many years ago, when Natasha had brought home Milly as a kitten, he had cut out the bottom of the conservatory door, and inserted a cat flap. This cat flap, like most, had a locking mechanism on it, allowing you the option to keep *The Cat* in or out.

Rick had watched with amusement as it had bolted through it, having never shown the slightest bit of interest before. But the moment that he flicked the little lever down, *The Cat* had dived through as though it had always been waiting for such a moment.

It had run up and down the lawn, jumping and twisting in the air. Then rolling its white body about on the lush summer green grass. It had looked to Rick like an oversized golf ball had come to life running about the green!

That first day Rick had decided to let *The Cat* roam, without any interruptions from him; he had no intentions of being an over-protective mother sort. But it had not travelled far, just meandering around the lawn, that living golf ball finding its new territory, catching the scent of rats and mice, future prey for its natural instincts.

On that particular sunny day, Rick had walked out onto the lawn. *The Cat*, having found its new spot on top of the shed's roof. Rick had at that moment felt it for the first time: terror, a primal fear, the unknown feeling of utter fear. His skin had crawled with unseen insects, the hair on the back of his head didn't just stand up it nearly jumped of his head. Yet he could not explain it, like when someone is walking behind you on a darkened street: they could be harmless, they might not.

Turning his head slowly, as though moving too fast would be dangerous, he had then seen *The Cat* looking at him. Sitting on the roof of the lead-shingled shed. Its tail flicking behind its head, green eyes glowing with dark perception burrowing into his own, seeking to find something.

He had looked away quickly, totally overawed by this sudden dumb-struck fear. He had stood gazing out towards his neighbour's garage. One mass of solid brick that had a tendency to block out the sun later on in the year.

Rick could hear the sound of the neighbour's koi fish pond, the motor droning like a car stuck in the first few seconds of a drag race, the constant bubbling that carried over the fence all year round.

Natasha had always hated that sound! So had he, now that he came to think of it. He had stood looking over towards the garage listening to the sound he had come to hate over the years.

Son of a bitch! That sound. Ten bloody years. To think the over-fed, over-paid guy pays a small fortune for that thing! If I could, I'd stop it once and for all I would. Just pull the goddamn plug! Whoosh!

The thought had been a childish one and Rick knew it, yet it had comforted him past the unknown fear; he was smiling again.

Turning back to his own garden, he noticed *The Cat*, on top of the shed roof, now standing on all fours, peering over towards the sound of the bubbling water.

Feel hungry? There is some mighty expensive sushi over the Berlin Wall, Buddy. Eat heartily!

The Cat turned, fixing its gaze on him.

Rick felt the insects start to crawl!

★ ★ ★

A rat, a big one, had been the first gift! In complete form, not a missing limb nor a mark on its rubbery skin.

Rick had been sipping black coffee, strong and hot, fingers burning on the mug. Walking across the lawn to say hello to *The Cat* who had left the house early, before even Rick had woken. Something that had not happened before, and even though he might not have admitted it to himself, like many things in his life, Rick could diagnose a man with pneumonia at twenty paces without speaking to him, but he would miss anything right under his own nose; he had been ever so slightly hurt, waking to find that where *The Cat* usually sat rubbing its nose on his, scratching gently at his face, there had been nothing but empty carpet.

Rick had nearly tripped over the rat's dead corpse!

It was in the centre of the green lawn. On its back, legs stiff, pointing up towards the blue, cloudless sky. Like dead twigs, twisted and brittle.

The Cat, sat upon its shingle throne, looking down on its generous gift.

Rick had had no intention of touching the dead rodent. His life often centred on the pain and suffering of others. But he did not want to feel the tight rubbery, skin of the dead rat on his fingertips.

Instead he had taken the rarely-used shovel from out of the shed. The stainless steel blade had shimmered in the brightness of the day.

The Cat laid its large white head upon its paws. Those two penetrating discs of green showing only the slightest interest in the proceedings that followed.

Rick had never had much interest in flowers or compost, yet the compliments that he had received in the past for the quality of his lawn had left a rather highbrow mark on him. So it was with great reluctance, Rick having been very pleased with the appearance of his lawn, that he put the virgin gardening tool to work.

The fine-soiled surface broke apart, the earth split beneath the cold steel, like trifle under spoon.

The task had not been as hard work as Rick had first feared; he rather enjoyed the feeling of having the sun on his back as he worked, and he rather felt that he could feel the calluses break under his soft skin. There was not much in the way of manual work in his day-to-day life.

He had liked it. Digging faster and faster. The hole had not been too deep. Two feet at the most!

After replacing the spade in the shed, stepping back out from under the shed, *The Cat* sitting above, the feeling of untold terrors struck once again.

He had nearly toppled with the force of it, like strong fingers against the temples pushing bony tips in hard. Fear and the inescapable feeling of being open, vulnerable.

Spinning on the spot, he had come directly under the gaze of the green eyes. He froze still, the heat of the day unable to account for the cold sweat creeping about his skin.

Then the feeling passed, almost as quickly as it had stamped down its appearance. There, looking up into *The Cat's* eyes, Rick felt subdued, the subtle sound of purring reaching his ears and then as if from out of the peripheral vision of his mind.

"You're welcome."

Rick knew that he hadn't heard anything, there was no one else in the garden, only himself. And he hadn't said anything. So it was just a mistake; he was catching the passing glances of some conversation, caught in a strong breeze

There had been no breeze, only the August heat hanging in the air.

The Cat had sat up, licked its left paw contentedly, then arched its back turned as if to walk away, but before Rick had lost sight of it, it cast him a quick sideways glance. Then it had been gone, in one quick leap of its hind legs, just a flash of white chased by morning shadow.

With this, thoughts more hectic than a motorway on the day before New Year Rick had retreated back to the conservatory, to refill his cup of coffee.

On returning to the conservatory, the sun beating down, warming his skin, he had placed the fresh mug upon the table. Leaning one hand against the conservatory window, the other tucked into the back pocket of his jeans, he watched for a long time. Until *The Cat* made its return.

There it had sat, its shingle throne warmed by the sun, looking back at Rick!

Rick scratched his chin, brow furred. Picked up his coffee and sipped through pursed lips. And before he could stop himself, before he could even account for why, he found himself thinking,

That's not the lot. No chance boyo!! There is more to this cat than you ever imagined!! He ain't no Aslan but I'm pretty sure he's not Garfield either!

* * *

The following morning, Rick left the house early. The street was the quintessential rural setting found throughout the Weepings. Containing mainly bungalows and the occasional three-bedroomed house set back a way from the quiet road with block-paved driveways, or stone chips for the not-quite-so -full-in-the-pocket type.

Rick lived in the end bungalow; the road being a dead end, there was very little traffic. This had been one of the main attractions for Natasha when they had moved from the three-bed apartment ten years ago.

The weather reached twenty nine degrees, the road glistened like it had been scattered with tiny diamonds. He drove slowly, no need to rush.

No need for anything really. Not any more.

He thought, as he turned the Honda Civic right at the end of the street. Warm rays of sunshine glared in through the windscreen; he slapped on the shades he kept in the car's glove box.

Today, is gonna be a good day!

When they had first arrived in the street all those years ago, Natasha had made the discovery of the small garden centre that made its business a couple of miles out of town.

The Civic pulled up into the car park; he closed the driver's door, relishing the heat of the day. His shoes made sharp, crunching sounds on the gravel beneath their soles. He liked that too.

The salesman had suggested an Uncle Dick! A substantial, standard, yellow-flowering rose. The perfect choice for a novice rose fancier.

Just the ticket!

The small mound of softened earth, raised up from where he had buried the rat, needed covering. Besides, he had done the same with Milly and he quite liked the idea now of adding some colour to the green garden.

As he pulled back onto his drive, there waiting on his doorstep, hands on hips, was an extremely overweight man. Whose neck seemed about ready to spill out over his shoulders like a water fountain. His legs, red and black, the muscles bruised with their strenuous daily job, were bare to the knees, his blue shorts far too small for a man of his size. On his head he wore large glasses that had slipped from his nose with the sweat that dripped from its tip. His face was red, not with sunburn, but from what could only be described as some acid reflux.

No, he is mighty pissed, and no prizes for guessing why!

The man was Rick's neighbour, Mr Dennis Pye. And before Rick had even shut the door of his car, rose tucked tight under his arm, he had seemed to charge down on Rick with an intention to carry out murder.

"How long have we known each other! How long! This is unacceptable, you know that. I'm not standing for it you know that don't you, you know that. |We have had this out before, haven't we! Don't you laugh don't you dare! Wipe that smile off your face!"

His voice was far too high-pitched for a man of his size, and had Rick not already harboured nothing but contempt for him, he would have found it difficult not to laugh at the reddened form of a Mr Dennis Pye.

"How can I help Dennis? Is this going to take long? Only I am a rather busy man."

Dennis interrupted with glee.

"Busy? Ha! Don't make me laugh, you haven't been busy for quite some time now, isn't that right?"

Rick made to brush past him, but the 300 pounds of stored carbohydrates moved to block his path. Rick, about ready to retaliate with his own outburst stopped, as from behind his back, Dennis brought forward a plastic bag, squashed and deformed with what looked like black slugs mottled in its bottom.

"I found this! This! On my pond's decking!!!

Rick was speechless,

"Cat droppings! Cat droppings! On my decking!"

Cat shit! Is this guy serious? He is thrusting cat shit at me!

Rick twisted past him. Dennis tried turning quickly to chase after him but stumbled and had to grab the bungalow's wall to steady himself.

"Listen, Dennis, I don't have a cat. Mine died remember, in the spring, I heard you celebrating over there, with your Tom Jones and your red wine and don't deny it"

"You're damn right I did, that dirty creature was always defecating on my decking, and now this, don't lie to me, I have heard you, out there at night, talking to it!"

Dennis's face was twisted into a smile now, it seemed more like a grimace to Rick, who felt slightly disturbed by its resemblance to the marshmallow man.

"Look Dennis, for the last time..."

"Don't lie! You're always lying! Well, we all know the truth. Yes, that's right Mr Big Shot we all know the truth, we know what really happened last year!"

The smile had turned into a full-time face splitter, red gums and black fillings cracked with sugar. Rick could feel the anger within him rising.

"Shut your pie hole, Dennis or I will knock those teeth down your fat throat!"

"Oh, don't you start that! You listen to me, we all know you killed her, you did it, yes we know. Don't think it's a big secret, we have your card. Oh yes."

With that, Rick dropped the plant, soil bursting out from its plastic container. He ran to be nose to nose with Dennis; the smell of gravy and chicken struck his nose like a right hook. But he didn't waver.

"Listen to me now, you bloody walrus! Get back in your house before I do something you'll regret!"

Dennis stared back, his eyes magnified by the thick lenses in his glasses, and for a brief moment Rick thought he might have a problem with the big guy. But Dennis's eyes fell to the floor, as they always had in any true sign of confrontation.

"That's what I thought, now get lost!"

Dennis shuffled off towards his front door, his ridiculous flip-flops barley keeping his fat feet from spilling him onto his side.

After watching Dennis all the way back into his house Rick picked up the broken plant pot, brushed the loose soil aside and went through his back gate into his garden.

There, he saw, standing on all four feet, *The Cat,* its countenance one of no interest, its green eyes wavering from Rick to the fence that bordered the line of the domestic war, which had been raging for a decade.

Rick felt sure that it had been listening, and as he made his way across the lawn towards the shed to fetch the spade, the invisible insects started to crawl over his skin once more.

He planted the yellow flowering rose over the grave of the dead rat.

No other rat in history has ever had such a burial.

It had added a bit of character to the bare lawn, Rick only now noticing that Milly's rose had given up the ghost. He hadn't noticed before; pangs of guilt tickled him as he turned his eye from the now-dead rose.

That evening was a peaceful one; Rick sat on the patio drinking a cool glass of beer, the air around him still mild and pleasant.

His feet stretched out and crossed at the ankles before him. The sun was just starting its decent form the sky. The beautiful reds of the sun filling him with tranquil, easy thoughts.

Those being a stranger over the past twelve months. Since Natasha had died.

His mind now started to wander, as it so often did with thoughts of her.

The Cat sat on the garden chair opposite him, the very chair that Natasha used to insist on having, on nights like this one.

She'd had green eyes! Beautifully green though, not like *The Cat's,* that seemed so dark and full of meaning. Sweetly green, like sparkling gems, left in the sunshine.

Rick, swaying with the effect of the beer, looked over at *The Cat,* who was looking back, never blinking, it always seemed to be thinking.

Then, with no warning, came the invisible insects again. His hair stood to attention on his neck, the skin on his palms became wet, the bottle of beer slipping from his hands.

There she sat, in her chair, the chair that she had so enjoyed on evenings like this in; as clear as day, there she sat before him!

Her brown curls pulled back behind small pale ears, freckles in the light of the evening, skin milky white. Her perfect chin sitting in her hands, the collar on her favourite cardigan pulled up to her cheeks, she had always been afraid of sudden weather changes.

Her hands reached out for Rick's across the table, her clubbed thumbs hidden from view, something she had always been very sensitive about, but that he had loved. Absurdly Rick felt shame then, for never telling how much he had loved her little clubbed thumbs, for not telling her about so many of the things that he loved about her.

He then heard, before he could move, or react in any way, somewhere in the far reaches of his mind, "Don't leave me, don't leave like the others have done!"

The bottle dropped, shattering into thousands of miniscule mirrors.

She was gone.

There only remained *The Cat*.

All was as it had been. The evening was turning chilly, the air crisper.

Rick could hear the sound of Dennis's pond, the motor a never-ending reminder of his hatred for the man.

Then another sound filtered its way through the drunken soup of sounds; *The Cat* was purring!

It jumped up from the chair, soft pads on the glass table top. Then jumped onto Rick's lap, making a deep purr from within its throat. It sat on Rick's stomach, rested its front paws on his chest and stared into Rick's eyes.

Rick suddenly felt very cold; the air seemed to turn to ice. But he didn't move. He just sat there looking back at *The Cat*; it seemed to Rick that he could meet his own past somewhere in those green pools of night.

"Hey boyo, if you keep purring like that you might just drown out the sound of that pond, and we wouldn't want that now, would we, boy?"

Rick laughed to himself.

That night as he lay with *The Cat* by his feet, Rick could have sworn that he could smell Natasha's perfume.

★ ★ ★

The next day Rick awoke, made himself a coffee, black with two sugars. The hangover was not as bad as he had expected.

He had smoky memories of the night before, nothing solid, wisps of dreams that he had a strange feeling he didn't want to remember.

He walked into the conservatory, well aware that for only the second time since bringing home *The Cat*, it was not following him about, with him nearly tripping on its tail, as had become the usual morning ritual.

He opened the conservatory door and walked out onto the patio.

Rick dropped the mug, its ringing smash lost in his muddled shock.

There lay, in the middle of the green lawn a soaking wet carcass. The ground about it stained red; blood leaked between the blades of grass, resembling spilled paint.

The koi carp was a big one; even Rick who had no interest in fish, could see that. He estimated it to be about twenty pounds, and two-and-a-half feet long.

Its stomach had been ripped apart, the intestines and swim bladder spilled across the lawn. Both eyeballs were missing.

The ground made dirty squelching and splashing noises as Rick's bare feet stepped doggedly towards the carnage. The pond water that had spilt from the fish had soaked the earth, its soil stained red.

The Cat sat on top of the shed. Its tail flicking behind its head, green eyes fixed on Rick.

Never blinking!

Rick watched as *The Cat* stood up, becoming a silhouette against the morning sun, the bristle along its back standing out like a cactus in the desert.

Shielding his eyes with his hand Rick watched as *The Cat* sauntered away across the roof of the shed. Yet, once again, before it was out of view, it stopped, yawned and cast a backwards glance towards Rick. The unwanted finger tips pressing at his temples with vigour.

"You're welcome."

Rick stood motionless, his eardrums ringing with the unwelcome voice inside his own skull.

★ ★ ★

The dead fish was a ghost koi carp, weighed eighteen pounds exactly, had been called Casper and happened to be Dennis Pye's pride and joy!

Dennis had paid £475 for it back in the summer of 2004, when it had measured no more than five inches long. He had paid extortionate amounts of money every year to have the pond's pump replaced. Even when this was not always needed, going to great lengths and precautions to make sure that the pond never become over-crowded. Allowing Casper to keep growing uninhibited by the other fish he had shared his home with.

There had been many a time in the past, when sitting out in the evenings, Rick and Natasha would sit quietly, glass of wine in hand, waiting for Dennis to come out to feed the jewel of his life.

'The Dennis Pye hour' Natasha had called it. Rick had often wondered just how far the obsession had gone.

Sitting there they would hear the sound of the whirring motor running the pond's pump, droning deeply like some far-off car alarm that everyone nearby can hear but can't do anything to stop. Then Dennis would make his appearance, his shuffling steps chugging their way across the wooden decking that surrounded his pond, the rattle-rattle-shake of the carp food in its cheap container, followed by his high-pitched voice, soft and comical.

"Casper, come Caspy Caspy, come to Dennis, Come to Dennis!"

Rick and Natasha stifled laughter under a clenched fist or handkerchief.

"Dennis loves Casper, doesn't he, yes he does, he loves all his fish but Caspy, he's the favourite. He knows Denny loves him."

Well, now Casper, the friendly ghost carp, was resembling some butchered pig, drip drying upside down. Its tail felt like a wet flannel, slippery and yet course, the slime excreted from the fish's scales finding the crooks of Rick's knuckles, wrinkling his fingers.

Casper's swim bladder and heart already lay below the dripping meat sack, in the three-foot hole. Rick had come to the conclusion that three feet was somehow more appropriate than two.

He stood, mud stains capped his jeans at the knees, while sweat dripped from his eyebrows and streamed down the lenses of his shades before finding the soil of the waiting grave.

For a time he froze, mid-stance, it was all Rick could do to keep his grip, the slime becoming a lather mixed with blood and perspiration. Looking down into the grave, he could see the grisly, dark-coloured heart seeming to look back up at him.

Rick just stood there, feet apart, Casper dangling and twisting on his own centre of gravity.

A warm August day, no different to any other!

He couldn't drop him, just couldn't do it. No matter how much he hated Dennis. And there was no chance, no chance that this fish, this gift, came from anywhere but next door, Rick couldn't fool himself on that.

Even so he just couldn't drop the fish. The very idea filled his mind with some idiotic idea of a courtroom, himself standing in the dock, muddy jeans and wet fingers that resembled crumpled lettuce.

NAME: Rick Cooper, Doctor

CRIME: The secret burial of a dead fish

EVIDENCE: It's three feet under my lawn, it's a nice lawn. Your honour! Honestly!

ANYTHNG TO ADD?: Yes, I can't find its eyeballs!

Rick found himself holding back a laugh, he didn't let it out, but he suspected that it might have been more of a hysterical cackle than a laugh.

The slime took its toll, Casper dropped, Rick's fist closing on slime, blood and sweat soup.

The sound was not unlike that of a water balloon falling on a mattress might make.

WOOLSHLOPP!

Casper spat blood and water from all openings. Rick filled in the hole.

The Cat was sitting over by the patio now, affording itself some shade from the ever-increasing heat of the day. Its green eyes not reflecting any sign of interest within.

Rick replaced the shovel back in the shed.

Now take a second here, Ricky boyo, that's one hell of a big fish! Could that cat really have killed it and dragged the damn thing over a six-foot fence and then onto the lawn?

Walking back over the blood and water-clogged patch where Casper's torn caucus had lain, Rick had to think, *It's alright I'll cut it short, real short, as short as the blades will go, the water and blood will soon drain away!*

He looked at The Cat. The Cat looked back. Rick half-relaxed from his recent exercise, half-poised ready for some reoccurring fear, the pain in the temples again.

"Casper, breakfast Casper." Shake, rattle, shake. "Caspy, it's breakfast time. Where are you hiding, Casper?"

Rick couldn't move, his muscles frozen solid, a lolly pop fresh out the freezer.

"Casper?"

There was panic now in the high-pitched tones, Rick could hear it. He had heard it many times before, had even used them himself in the not-so-distant past.

"Casper, stop fooling about, breakfast, Caspy."

Rick couldn't help the way his lips curled into a smile. Not a big one, just as small one, not a winner just a teeny-weeny smirk.

He did feel for Dennis, but he couldn't help that cream-filled tart, sat amongst the sugar-free ones. He hadn't taken a bite yet, just had a good look.

As Rick walked back into the house, *The Cat* jumped too and followed suit.

I wonder now, pink. I like the colour pink, I will ask the girl in the garden centre, the one with the nose ring, I'll ask her if she has any late-flowering, pink roses; should cheer the place up a bit.

The conservatory door closed, shielding Rick's ears from the desperate cries of Dennis that carried in the air louder than any car alarm.

* * *

Over the following week Rick ran his mind over the whole Casper situation regularly, like a saw run through wood. He never could make any sense if it.

He had managed to convince himself that *The Cat* had not purposely killed the fish, that it had all been a coincidence. *The Cat* had found the fish dead, washed up against the edge of the pond's wall maybe, or perhaps some large bird of prey had killed it and not realised the magnitude of its kill, abandoning it for any innocent cat to find on its travels.

As for not being able to carry it, well he had seen many wildlife shows, wild big cats carrying prey three, sometimes four, times their own weight. Was it really that much of a stretch to think that *The Cat*, which happened to be larger than most domestics, had managed this feat, dragging the fish from its dark wet home.

Sawing through this piece of wood thick with confusion in his mind, he had managed to divert the blade from the ultimate question.

Why? Why that fish? Why had he chosen that fish and left it there for him to find? Dennis had markedly avoided him since the secret burial.

No he's not, you just hate each other, it was only the day before the beached whale was found that the two of you had almost cut up rough on the driveway, you're being paranoid, he's hardly going to wave with a smile and prayer after that, is he?

But even so, Rick had also made no attempts to make contact his neighbour, keeping the blinds drawn, sneaking peeks, making sure the coast was clear before leaving the house.

He pondered for some time about Dennis. The time that Milly had come crawling back through the cat flap, blood streaked out behind her like some red slug had followed her home. It had taken Natasha hours to dress the wounds. Dennis had set razor wire, sharp and twisted in its rusted lengths, on the roof of his garage. Rick remembered how Natasha had to restrain him, had to keep him from breaking the guy's face with her rolling pin she had been baking with at the time.

When Rick's bubble of thought found its way to Natasha, it had a tendency to meander, of course, a speeding car taking a slip road to some quieter area of the mind.

He wondered how Natasha would feel about Casper's fate. Being a vet had kept the fire of love she had for animals well-lit for the years they had been married. They had both laughed and scoffed at the crazy man next door and his noisy fish pond.

Yet somehow he didn't think she would have been particularly impressed. The carcass of Dennis's whole life lying on their lawn, eyeless and heartless.

Don't think she would have liked that, Buddy! Don't think she would have been impressed one bit!

The car would then make its way back to the cluttered motorway, all manner of questions scrambling for the fast lane.

Had the cat done it on purpose? Could it have? It had obviously seen the way we had argued, but seriously, a cat that held a grudge? That's some serious shit!

But there had been other niggling doubts; the way *The Cat* had stretched out on the lawn, rolling and turning as he had planted 'white delight', the new white petal rose, planted above the late Casper the Great.

Purring so loudly, Rick had been sure Dennis would hear and, by some unbelievable sense, discover the whole sordid business.

Later on that night, *The Cat* had been overly affectionate, annoyingly so. Mewing and rubbing its head on his legs, nearly tripping him twice in its attempt to be near him. Had it been Milly behaving so, he would have removed her, locking her away in the one of the upstairs rooms until she had calmed herself down. Not this cat, he couldn't bring himself to scold it, nor shout or discipline it, not with the way the deep green eyes would fixate on him with shades of the deepest love and tenderness. As all pet owners know, there are some types of affection that only a beloved pet can provide.

The week had not been uneventful; *The Cat* had brought him two gifts, if not quite so tongue-in-cheek. Rick had never seen a hare before; it had saddened him, the way the blood smelt, the neck ripped back to the bone, the head connected by only a small flap of skin and brittle bone.

Again *The Cat* had sat upon the shed's roof, watching the proceedings with mild, unflattering interest. For this particular grave, Rick had chosen a deep-red coloured shrub rose, it had a far denser amount of thorns than any of the others; blood seeped from cuts that the plant's defences had made in his skin.

He had chosen a boxwood plant, cut into the shape of a man wearing a hat and holding a cane, to sit over the grave of the crow. It had impressed him, the jet-black feathers and large bony beak. He had unbelievably expected the bird to bleed black blood, like spilt ink. But it had been only red, the same as any other murdered creature.

During these little incidents he became consumed with the feeling of guilt, that he should, in some way, be punishing *The Cat*, stopping this unnecessary slaughter of animals. Yet he could never rid himself of the sugar-crammed, calorie-bulging tart, the one that seemed to coo in a female voice over the savoury, boring tarts.

There's no need to be mad! It's just a way of showing his affection, cats aren't dogs; they don't lick and jump. Just take the compliment.

Besides, he had come to the conclusion, all in all, the garden looked a lot more attractive with the new flowers in it.

★ ★ ★

Sabena Jackson was the only real Hollywood beauty in the Weepings. Oh, there were other beautiful women, young and old. But there was only one Sabena.

The morning was hot, reaching 29 degrees, her slight red dress slipping about her delicious body taking on her curves and emphasising the smoothness of her skin. She couldn't remember a warmer summer, and that suited her just fine.

Her high heels were not appropriate any more than the well-above-the-knee dress, but Sabena didn't mind. This was just how she liked it. She had moved onto the street six months ago from another town, somewhere near the sea.

The click of her heels followed by the dancing perfume that radiated about her presence was enough to turn any man's head, let alone her prefect shape.

Her behind moved with an exaggerated shuffle and her shoulders were almost swinging with her stride.

This was one smoking-hot lady. Hollywood certainly had come to the Weepings.

Usually she would not be out walking that early; as a rule Sabena didn't like to get out of bed before 10am at the weekend. But today was different, the warmth of the morning had dragged her by the arm and pulled her onto the street. Besides, Rinty needed walking.

Rinty was Sabena's five-year-old pet poodle. His fur had been died pink, he wore a pink collar that was connected to Sabena by a thin-corded purple lead. The dog was a toy poodle, and he suited his mistress in every way imaginable.

Rinty, as always, walked in front of his mistress - training was not part of his daily routine - wiggling his absurdly coloured tail as he strode ahead.

Sabena had walked the usual route, little Rinty's favourite, up past the centre and past the many people out on the summer's day shopping; she had enjoyed the many looks and expected grins from men, the frustrated and envious glances of the women. This morning was a good morning for Sabena.

She was nearly home when Rinty pulled hard and yanked the girly lead from her hand. He ran off down towards the bottom of the cul-de-sac. Barking his little pink head off as he went. Tail waving from side to side. He had seen something, something that he could not resist. His instincts had taken over.

Sabena, hobbling on her high heels, gave chase after her little friend. A very comical sight for a Sunday morning in the Weepings, one that made many blinds along the street flicker.

"Rinty!!Come back here Rinty, you little shit, come back!"

The dog's barking gave way to another noise. The high-pitched squeal and rattle of a fight, the only noise that could ever sound so aggressive is that of an animal fight.

Panic made its way to Sabena, she may have him wearing a girl's collar and died his fur pink, but she did love the little dog. When she finally made it to the last house on the road she found her dog in a stand-off with a large, white cat. A cat that seemed to be as big as Rinty himself, with deep green eyes and a lion's mane about its neck. Sabena had never before seen such a cat in her life; it fair took her breath away. She stood lead hanging limply in one hand, her weight unsteady on her heels, watching as the dog slowly backed away from the snarling cat. It hissed and growled deep down in its throat. It seemed that this cat had been a bit more than the little dog had expected.

"Come away now, Rinty. Come on now hun, let's leave the nasty old cat alone shall we? There's a good boy!"

Her voice was uncertain, it may well have been a tiger standing before her in the Indian jungle. This was most definitely out of character for her morning walk, and she did not like it, not one bit.

Rinty backed away, keeping his eyes on the creature before it, the dog was not growling, it made no noise whatsoever, its left ear was ever so slightly torn; blood trickled from the cut.

Just as she managed to get a hold of Rinty, placing his lead on his collar, a man came round from the back of the house.

"Is everything alright...? Oh, hello."

Rick was taken by surprise to find Sabena on his front lawn. He took the sight of her in, the way her golden hair was tied backwards into a plait laying across her right shoulder, her sunglasses making her look like a movie star. The Don Henley song popped into his head,

I can see you... you got your hair tied back and your sunglasses on.

This is not the time for Don Henley!

Sabena knew Rick; they had some time the previous year, she had forgotten when exactly, been on a disastrous date. Enough said!

"Oh, it's you is it? Well, is this thing yours?"

Her voice was full of hard breaths from her exertion, making her ample and implanted breasts heave beneath the revealing dress, something Rick couldn't help but notice.

"Err, yeah, that's my cat."

The Cat was walking between Rick's feet, back arched and purring, its tail wrapped around his left knee; he tried to push *The Cat* away, rather embarrassed.

"Yeah, that's my cat alright. I'm sorry, what happened Sabena?"

"Well that animal of yours has injured my poor Rinty, here, look!"

She held Rinty in her arms holding the ear out for the whole world to see, the pink fur a strong contrast to the light red of her dress.

"I'm sorry, he has never done anything like that before. But I think it's more likely that it was that dog of yours! Let's not forget he used to have a habit of chasing my other cat!"

Sabena stepped forward, her unpleasant feeling from earlier had passed; she felt foolish and a little silly at how *The Cat* had made her feel. Now the guns were coming out. Both barrels!

"Look here, Mr Doctor, I don't care if he used to chase some mangy cat, this here is a pedigree, you know what that means, do ya?"

"Yeah Sabena, I know what that means. I also know that that dog is a menace. Can you get it to shut up!"

Rinty, now safe from *The Cat*, was emitting short barks, loud enough to wake the dead. He was a brave wolf once again.

"Don't you speak to me like that! I suppose it's all his fault now then is it? Look at his ear!"

"Ok Sabena, I'm very sorry about Rinty's ear. But if you kept him under a bit of control then perhaps the little rat wouldn't get into trouble!"

Rick was tired of this; he had had enough. Sabena was good to look at, but he found out last year that she was not as nice inside. He had turned to her at a time when he was at his lowest after Natasha's death; he had needed someone, turning to Sabena even though it was a mistake. It had been one drink in the local pub. She had left when his one had turned into six, but not until after he had learned enough to know he didn't care.

"What! Don't call him a rat! What? Is this because of me walking out on you? Is that it, Doctor? You think that you can embarrass me. I'm not the one who should be embarrassed now, should I!"

She walked forward with Rinty held in her arms; she leant towards Rick, her blue eyes that he had once found so attractive, but now made him squirm, peered out from over the top of her Raybans!

"You think it's a big secret do you?"

Her sweet, minty breath teased the skin on his face, her perfume drilled his mind with the colour pink. He had, at one time, wished for her body to be close to his. Well, she was close to him now, close enough for her to whisper.

"We all know what you did. There are no secrets here, Mr Doctor man!

She giggled, her teeth were perfect piano keys glinting in the sunlight.

"It's all over the town. We all know!"

Rick had a sudden urge to smash those piano keys into a thousand pieces and stomp them into dust.

"Hey look, I was just going to say…"

"I don't give a shit what you were going to say. Just remember what I have said there are no secrets here, you must know that. Now now, Rinty stop that barking, the drunken doctor doesn't like it much!"

She smiled again; her sunglasses were now on the end of her nose!. She cast a sweeping glance over at Rick's Honda perched on the driveway.

"Make sure to sound the horn, Babe, when you reverse out, want to give us all a chance at least, don't you?"

She leant closer now, almost nose to nose with Rick. He held his breath so she wouldn't notice the smell of beer, her perfume seemed to consume him.

"Don't want any more accidents now, do we Doctor?"

Right then, Rick wished the perfume would consume him, like a puff of smoke, just send him away. Anywhere but there, in the hot summer's sun in front of that women, in front of the street that he knew would be watching from behind net curtains and Venetian blinds.

"I don't like you speaking to me, so you just remember that, and keep that filthy cat away from Rinty!"

With that, she turned, walking away down the street, the click of her heels a gong echoing inside his skull.

Rick stood still, both hands clenched into tight fists, he felt as though the only thing that he could do right then, right in that moment, was to scream, to scream after her and vent twelve months' hatred and frustration, let it all just run out of him! But he didn't. He just stood still, secretly glad that he was wearing his shades so that the people behind their curtains and blinds wouldn't see the tears steal their way down his face and onto his lips.

The Cat sat between his feet. It sat still. Very still, the green eyes followed the lady down the street as she walked away. Its eyes burned a darker shade of green, a flame flicked there. It's purring had turned to a deep growl that vibrated in the air.

Rinty the dog looked back, its eyes on *The Cat*. Its short barks stopped, becoming a painful whining noise, not unlike that of a crying child.

Rick sat on the wooden stool in his kitchen, the whiteness of the tiles raked at his eyeballs, the wood beneath him groaned with his weight.

His clothes felt too tight. Pressing in on him from all sides.

The air was thick.

He sat still, knuckles whitened by his grip on the edges of the stool's rounded seat. He sat still, waiting for the rain to come. August rain, a grey cloud suspended over Doctor Richard Cooper's bowed head.

The tears fell and fell, his shoulders shook with violent vigour. He didn't moan or sob. Just cried. Cried unconditionally. This heartache needed no dramatics!

He cried, he cried so hard that he didn't notice *The Cat* walking over to his feet, circling him like some albino lion circling his trainer in some long bye-the-bye circus tent.

Rick's mind raced with thoughts of Natasha and that last night that they were together. The rain, the darkness of the tarmac stretched out before him, the wipers beating on the windscreen, the sound they had made. The coolness of the steering wheel under his fingers.

The Cat stopped circling. Reared up, placing its front paws on his lap, his jeans damp with the sadness that leaked from his eyelids.

The green eyes locked onto his, delving deep into his sorrow, never blinking, it seemed, always thinking.

Rick could see it all so clearly, that night laid out before him, some re–run of a bad movie he would watch as a kid.

He could see her, sweet Natasha, sat next to him in the passenger seat which had been pulled back, her head lolled against the head rest, her eyes closed in sleep. Things came back to him, things that he had forgotten with time, she had looked as though she had been dreaming, her eyelids betraying slight movements underneath.

I wonder what she had been dreaming.

The trust in the half-smile that curled on her cherry lips, red with the night's gloss.

Then black, dark, noise, sirens, blotted by drops of inky confusion on the smudged paper of his mind. Then it was gone. He was back in the kitchen, the stool creaking with contempt, his shoulders slowed in their movement.

And *The Cat*. Looking up at him. Something new made its way out of those green eyes. Love. Simple unstoppable love. *The Cat* purred. Rick held it to his chest, the white fur soothing his shaky state of mind.

Thank God for you, Buddy! Thank God for you, thanks for being here!

As the two of them, man and beast, cemented their connection that day, Rick found his day followed by a dreamy state of lamented peacefulness.

As he said good night to *The Cat* that night his eyelids were heavy with alcohol-induced fatigue. He looked at it, and felt that feeling of panic, the fingers of fear pressing at his temples again. Only this time he didn't flinch, this time, stroking *The Cat*, he simply let it pass. The animal looked away from him as though unaware of his presence.

Then a thought emerged in the most secret part of Rick inner self. A thought that he would never tell a living soul, a thought so outrageous and impossible he didn't give it much of a chance to grow. Instead he rolled over on his pillow and considered it.

Well, let's just see what tomorrow brings.

★ ★ ★

Rinty's basket was as fine as they come! Cross-chequered with pink and puce squares.

The air was filled with all manner of fragrances, perfume for all the different nights and all the different occasions.

Sabena's bed sat against the white-wallpapered wall nearest the en-suite bathroom door. Above this bed, about four feet from the pink tweed dog bed, there was an open window, the frilly lace curtains danced to an unheard tune in the late-night breeze.

The room itself was not overly big. Yet in many ways it resembled its occupant. Open, spacious, pretty, photos all framed in black, scattered about the white walls, photos of herself and college friends from years ago. Some were from a holiday with an old boyfriend who had insisted on making her walk all over the world.

There were absolutely no photographs of family.

A wooden dressing table, milky white, was close by the bed, mobile phone sitting on top, charging ready for some emergency call from a superficial friend. Ring towers, five of them, covered from top to bottom in sparkling bands of silver were close by.

Jewellery boxes, some new, some old, filled any possible empty space. The wardrobe, doors mirrored, was one of those large sliding affairs; its door stood open, clothes spread out across the room's floor. Shoes of all shapes and sizes, some in their original boxes, never opened, lay on top of one another in the corner furthest from the door.

Sabena lay asleep, her ample chest lowered and raised, breathing through her slumber, dreaming. The dreams were always unpleasant as well as alarming. Usually she would toss and turn, sometimes so violently she would pull the covers off herself. Twice she had flung herself completely out of bed, landing on the bedroom floor with a dull thud, her eyes opened wide, ears echoing with the sound of Rinty's alarm at her outburst.

Most frustrating of all, the dream was nearly always the same, with only ever-so-slight altercations, the smallest of details changed. She would be dreaming of warmth and sunlight, strobes and flashes of fresh air hitting her face, the sound of a familiar voice in the world around her. The alien state of dreaming, twisting and turning her in the scene from the past. The scene was a sandy beach; she knew the beech but dare not think of the name.

Then the dream would change, as quickly as it would start. There was coldness about her, the smell of salt thrown up her nose, she felt unable to breath, the light had turned grey, dark clouds in a dark, fear-filled dream.

Then the sound she feared the most, breaking its way out through the dream's wall of protection, turning it into the worst of nightmares, the same nightmare she had had every day for years.

The sound was always the same, the sound of that familiar voice, crying, crying out for her. The sound chilled her heart, the skin she was encased in, conscious and unconscious bursting out in baths of sweat.

In the dream, the smell of salt made its way to taste; she couldn't breathe, there was no light any more, only darkness and soul-shaking fear.

And that would be that. She would wake. She would usually find it hard to adjust back to the reality of consciousness. Head pounding. She would, in her lonely state, try to calm herself. We all have those moments, moments when we are totally and utterly left open to attack, when we let all barriers down and, for that one moment, no matter how old we are, we long for the hand of a loved one to reassure us.

It's all alright! It's all alright, nothing to be scared of here!

After these nightmares Sabena would be breathing hard, waiting for Rinty, who would trot over to his mistress and lick her face, jumping onto her lap and snuggling his head against her chest. The sort of comfort only a pet can provide, there is always a hidden figure at the back of human's sympathy, that figure is called pity. Pets have no such figure in their make-up. They love and they love completely.

And so she would usually sit with Rinty in her lap soaking up the offerings of emotional support he offered with his unconditional support. The dream was nearly always the same.

Not tonight. Tonight was very different indeed!

Her scream was short and desperate, followed by a quick covering of the mouth with her delicate hands. Her lungs raged with their function.

The dream was so vivid, even now it seemed to cling to her; she shook her arms and flung her hands about her head, eyes now snapped shut. She tried to shake of the invisible trace left by the nightmare.

She had not been herself, she had somehow in the world of dreams left her curvy, well-exercised figure behind. She was something else, something small, fidgeting and hot; thirst ravaged her small throat.

Even in her new, small body she was still in her bedroom, looking around with keen, expert eyes. She was Rinty, she had become Rinty in the dream.

The duvet clutched in her grip became the stress relief valve she so longed for. The dream made its way back to her, she was not allowed to forget.

She had been afraid, her whole body, small and hot with the permed fur that covered it, fear had filled her, clouding out all other senses! She was sat in the basket, the bed basket that belonged to her dog. She had sat there, looking up past the face of herself in bed sleeping soundly and, above her, the window.

Open.

Sabena always slept with the window shut, she hated to feel breeze when she slept, had done ever since her college days.

Her vision had been different in the dream, hazy smouldering grey shapes, highlighted in green wisps.

As she sat in the basket, her throat feeling sore with thirst, she was aware that something was outside the window. As Rinty, she knew this. But dared not make a sound. The heart inside her chest, small and desperate with terror, beat fast and to no rhythm. She was panicking. She had wanted to bark, to bark loudly and scream her little lungs out, but no noise came.

The window had opened!

The eyes that looked down at her were not human, they couldn't have been. Sabena knew that.

They weren't animal either! Rinty knew that!

Nothing but the bottom depths of the most pained soul and nightmare could cough up so vile a vision as that which stared down onto her face.

The face hung down from the sill, moving slowly, there seemed to be hot breath emanating from its teeth, as Rinty she looked frantically at her sleeping owner, who seemed unaware that this monster passed inches from her.

Bat's ears, hazy and incoherent with the dream's smoked vision grew high over a long serpent's face, diamond-shaped green eyes burned into her fear.

A python's set of silky fangs parted into a grin, a forked red tongue licked her furred face, and the smell of its breath drove the sandpaper in her throat to shuffle in the attempt to scream.

With that, Sabena had woken. Steadying herself, she leant her head back, breathing hard. She placed her hand on her heaving breasts.

She looked for Rinty in his basket, which of course was empty.

The breeze from the open window ruffled her hair. Her gaze fell on the open space there above her dog's bed, killing a piece of her already-lonely heart.

She had locked it before bed. She always did. Hated feeling a breeze at night. Had done since college.

Her head fell between her knees as she realised, not for the first time in her life, that she was very much alone in her fear.

★ ★ ★

The morning that followed was not a pleasant one for most. The weather had broken that night. At one in the morning, the rain had fallen. True August rain, covering the whole of the Weepings.

Rick woke, the rain peppering his window. His stomach brought nausea to his head. He really had fallen to the bottle the night before, after the bitter encounter with Sabena.

Slumping onto the sofa of the conservatory, temples feeling like they had been used to jam a revolving door, he stretched out his feet before him.

The reflection in the window before him did not pull any punches.

Great! Forty-two years old and you can't handle a hangover. After all the practice you get, boyo you should be a bloody expert!

This was no simple hangover, no chance. Had he had time to look outside, he would have seen strewn about the patio, evidence of his escapade. One hell of a tin mountain, with an empty bottle of red thrown in, that his parents had given him years ago, it had been well past its use-by date, but by that time Rick's ship of self-recreation had well and truly sailed, full sail and gusto!

Struggling to wake the memories of the previous night, like maggots they steadily began to crawl up through his battered memory bank.

Then, for the first time he realised something, something important. Where was *The Cat*? Usually by now it would be clawing up at his legs, mewing loudly, not as had occurred to Rick in the past, for food or treats as most cats do. Crafty felines that desire one thing, treats.

Where are you, Buddy?

Then the maggots reached the top of the memory bank. It all came back to him. The meeting with Sabena in the street, the way he cried afterwards, the way he had so vividly been taken back to the night of Natasha's death. And he remembered the thought he had had last thing that night when, drunk and clumsy, he had fallen to sleep.

Fragments of a distorted dehydrated idea fired up in his head. A crazy idea, something that he dare not even consider for the sake of his own sanity.

His palms started to sweat.

He sat forward, looking past the hollow reflection that mimicked him, looking out past the patio and the tin mountain, past the upturned chair that he remembered falling out of as the ship sailed into the sunset; he stared right out into the garden.

It was now, for the first time, that he noticed the rain on the streaked window, blurring that aging reflection, something for which he was secretly glad.

And there, out passed the lawn and recently planted headstones, sat *The Cat*!

On top the shed, on its shingle throne it rested. Its figure blurred by the morning downpour. Bringing to mind images of lions on the Serengeti, the faces hazed by the heat of the day captured by some keen movie maker.

Rick's sweaty palms clasped the cool wicker armrests, lifting his weight he walked to the sliding door.

He opened it, the squeal of the door's roller wheels louder than it should have been in his drunken state.

It would have been a lie to say that Rick had been completely surprised. That on opening the door he had expected the scene before him to be what anyone would expect to see.

But that was not the truth. Not on your nelly!

Rinty's body resembled diced beetroot. Clumps and bumps mottled with smatterings of fur. Patches of this mottled pink fur scattered the garden, like sodden paper after a party.

The dark, red blood had nowhere to drain on the rain sodden lawn, shaping out around the deformed body a puddle of Rinty stew.

There was a smell scraping at his nose hair.

Rick stumbled, just catching himself on the patio table, saving his fall.

This was bad, very bad. But to look at *The Cat* you wouldn't have thought so. Sincere nobility, Sir Cat, enjoying a spot of summer rain. Just the ticket.

Rain clung to his chest hair, water splashed between his toes as he walked to the scene of the crime. His hangover was gone, one hell of a funny cure.

Rain threatened his vision, eyelashes sodden wet. Rinty's remains lay before him, the dog's dead tongue poking out from its lifeless mouth.

Christ, its tongue looks like a shitting slug, a slug deciding whether or not to enter. A bloody slug. Christ! This is bad. Do not throw up! Do not, do not throw up!!

The chunks of wet fur that had been torn from the little dog's body had left open patches of skin, revealing huge slices of bloodied bone.

The ground around the remains, although flooded with rain-red stew, had been churned up to a pulp. Rick took this in.

Oh boy, oh boyo, looks like little Rinty esquire was still kicking when he got here. Christ, this is bad, this is bad!

He drew his eyes up towards *The Cat*, laying on the shed, the drumming of the rain not deterring it in the slightest. Its massive head resting on its solid front paws! Tail flicking behind its head. The tail, it seemed to Rick, had changed shape, as though overnight it had grown thicker and longer, it was shaped differently at the tip.

Rick looked about at the thorn-covered headstones, bits of Rinty's pink perm snagged on the rose's thorns. He turned back to *The Cat*,

What in the name of God are you?

The Cat raised its head, its green pools of deception burning bright through the dreary atmosphere, forever staring, never blinking, always thinking.

Rick looked down at the sopping remains.

Perhaps I should try some kind of tree this time?

★ ★ ★

Mr Dennis 'who ate that' Pye had not always been overweight. To Dennis, his current physical condition was far more appalling to himself than it could ever be to some bystander on the street.

He hadn't always been so, in his first year at university back in '86, he had been the best damn squash player the university had ever had, winning numerous tournaments, university cups and leagues. The

University of Loughborough had thrown him into as many competitions as he could handle, not to mention cross-country runs and half marathons.

At one point, when the work load had piled up and he had found it hard to juggle life as a student with learning to survive in the world, he had considered giving up his future in business accountancy altogether. He had seen himself as a professional squash player, bright lights, trophies and ribbons cut by glamorous women. Maybe even hitting the world leagues?

He had, of course, done nothing of the kind. He had been, still was, a very sensible person.

A very insecure person.

He lived comfortably enough; the reason for such was his acumen with figures. He possessed an extraordinary ability to translate these to business matters. He was an accountant. A good one, at that.

He graduated in the year of '89, and at the age of 23, the world had been his to tame. He had been offered a job in Loughborough for a food commercial company, heading the accounts department which had consisted of himself and a middle-aged secretary called Mary.

He had stayed three years, it hadn't been that he was unhappy, but Dennis Pye was a clever man, and that sort of intelligence can tire easily with boredom.

It was in the summer of '91 that he received a phone call from a man calling himself Boston.

"Hello, is that Mr Dennis Pye?" the voice on the end of the line had said, short and brusque.

"Err, yes, who's calling?"

"Your future, Mr Pye!"

Turned out his old lecturer at university had been to local business meetings, the kind where suits, bulging at the waistband, meet to shake hands and fan already-burning egos.

There the lecturer had been asked, "I'm looking for a guy who works with the business matter, the index and figures, without trying to change the damn thing."

To which the lecturer replied instantly, I know just the man."

And so that, as is so often the case, in the world of four-figure and sometimes six-figure sums, is how Dennis had found himself speaking to Mr Boston.

"Future, I'm sorry I don't understand? Are you sure you have the right number, I'm Loweston Road."

"Mr Pye, not any more, you're not!"

Three weeks later, after a rather relaxed interview with the owner of Baker Works, Charles Boston, Dennis had found himself staring at the back of a removals van with Quick Moves written in bold red paint staring right back at him. On his way to take up his new position as production accountant, at the well-established company that supplied bakery machines all over the world. The factory was stationed on the edge of a little, sleepy market town called The Weepings, where he had found himself a bungalow in a cul-de-sac named Water's Bridge.

He had started his new position on a salary of £15,000, a lot of money for a 26 year-old, unmarried man! And that was that, as they say.

Promotion followed pay rise followed promotion. His career was a full success; Charles Boston never had reason to regret his decision.

Eventually as time trickled away down that never-ending slope of life, Dennis felt that niggle, that scraping little feeling, depression, poke its ugly head up from the soil of his life. And with the feeling growing into a full-blown weed of lonely self-hate, so did the inches about his waist grow with it.

His weight increased steadily but with deadly force, showing no signs of stopping, the drinking of whisky crept up on him like a nightmare to a light sleeper, the only thing that seemed to numb the pain in his eyes when they found his reflection.

The few friends he had managed to scrabble together at Baker Works married, had kids, divorced or, for reasons of their own, began to shun him.

It was then, one spring day, alone, the TV droning in the background, that Dennis realised he was an alcoholic, as well as a 'foodoholic'.

Whisky had become the crutch the runner needs after an irreversible accident. It was during this time that he cried himself to sleep, there were no longer any mirrors in his house. The world of sleep only a passing painkiller to his everyday life.

One day, a day which he remembers more vividly than any in his life, he had been to a colleague's house, on business; no one had socialised with Dennis 'who ate the' Pye for a long time. He had stepped out into the garden, scotch in hand, hearing the noise of the pond that he remembered practically filled the whole garden.

He had just, stood glass in hand, mesmerised by the fish swimming within.

By the end of the month he had a twenty-foot-by-twelve pond built with surrounding decking. and patio bar. He purchased four fish, expensive fish. Only the best for Dennis. They had cost £2,125 sterling!

"A real snip!" the breeder had coughed, between puffs of a cigar.

Amongst the four koi carp, he had picked one specifically, at only five inches long, the silver-backed, grey-finned ghost koi had been no bigger than a goldfish. But Dennis had loved him from first sight.

That fish he had called Casper! Without even knowing it Casper had saved Dennis's life. Suicide had tempted Dennis Pye more times than he dared think in the few years preceding his spontaneous purchase.

Casper couldn't save him from the two litre bottle of coke, or the Jim Bean 'let's get mighty mean' glass of scotch. No, I'm afraid that train had left the station many years ago and was rushing its way closer to the next station, heart failure, every day!

But Dennis had found something in the sound of the bubbles, and the hum of the motor: contentment. Rain or shine he could sit on the heated decking, money was no object, listening and watching the movements of the fish, his very own echo system. If Dennis had got himself a counsellor, they might have said it was therapeutic for him. All Dennis cared about was that he felt a warm glowing happiness in the presence of that pond. It made him happy. Casper especially.

But now Casper was gone!

Worse still he had no idea where or what had happened to his white knight. There had been dregs and small snatches of artificial weed lying about the decking, his panicking and pain-stricken eyes had been sure they had seen whispers of them on the fence, that kept the border between him and the doctor neighbour.

Dennis had made a full inspection of all his property, its walls and gates, even checking for traces of fish slime on the tops of the wooden fence. He had done this at night with a torch when he knew the doctor would be inside. But that day it had rained hard, washing away any evidence he could have found, or that might have been there, to give him even the slightest of clues as to what had happened to his friend.

No one had tried to break in! He was sure of that! No cat, even the biggest, could have managed to carry an eighteen pound carp, let alone carry it over a fence or brick wall!

Dennis sat now on his patio, listening to the calming bubble of the pond's motor, delivering white charges of oxygen to his remaining fish.

His eyes were grey with lost emotion, he had cried. Cried for Casper, the fish, that deep down even he knew had kept him from making some drunken drastic decision over the last eleven years.

Fat fingers tightened, blisters of white fat showed under the red skin, on his scotch glass.

He knew it had been him! That moronic doctor next door, the crazy drunk that had killed his own wife last year in some drunken car accident.

Oh, you got away with things when you had position didn't you! That doctor! He was twisted, unhinged after what had happened to his wife.

There's no doctor worse than a drunk doctor, he mused quietly to himself. Swaying gently in his seat.

"He ain't ever liked me, just like the rest of them!" He sniffed in air through his nose, stifling a sob that would have made him spill the Jim Beam from the glass.

"He did it! I know he did it!"

With that, the glass splintered into sharp pieces, the dark liquid reddening the clean wood under his socked feet. He winced, sucking his bleeding fingers, the pain dulled by the 40% drink.

"Oops, looks like I need a doctor after all!"

He laughed thinly as he sat there, letting the blood from his finger mix with the wasted scotch.

His mind didn't usually find aggressive or unfriendly thoughts, but right then, under the shade of his canopy roof with bleeding finger and sorrow-strained eyes, he managed well enough.

★ ★ ★

The Cat rubbed its head on Rick's legs, mewing and purring its happiness.

Rick sipped his tea through stubble-strewn lips, standing in the conservatory, his favourite place to think, leaning one shoulder against the sliding door. He held apart the blinds, like some Peeping Tom out for a kick. He had chosen a dogwood plant for the dog's headstone, it seemed rather fitting, all in all.

The small, lightly-green-coloured foliage was unable to hide the deep reds of the stems delivering their sustenance beneath. They reminded him somewhat of the bloody pulp buried under its roots.

Letting the blinds snap shut, placing the steaming cup aside, he looked down at the fingers of both hands held up before his face. They were shaded brown with the toils of the work he had done in the rain. Darkened streaks of dirt lined the creases of his hands' skin, black roads on a map.

The TV that hung on the wall to one side of the sliding door announced the start of QI.

Nice, I'm just about in the market for a good laugh!

The Cat, jumping onto his lap, made it quite clear that he was not impressed with this change in Rick's attention, who would by this time in the evening have sore knees from playing 'chase the white lion'!

Rick's face was irritated by the fur being rubbed in his face. Pushing *The Cat* away with the back of his hand, the confusion of the day giving way to impatience, *The Cat* landed on the floor, like all cats on its feet. It turned on Rick, fur raised along the arch of its back, sharp fangs bared, pink tongue flared in anger. It's hissing drowned out the sound of Steven Fry.

The fingers of fear probed the insides of Rick's temple once again. His eyes stung with sudden pain like a whole season's episode of hay fever constricted to a few seconds. The skin on the back of his neck went cold his own hair standing prompt.

Christ! What the hell was that!

His head then seemed to clear, the pain passing with a dull throb, he rested his elbows on the mud stained knees of his jeans. Dirt-streaked hands holding his forehead. *The Cat*, standing looking up at him, the green eyes seemed over powered by black pupils that reached out into Rick's fear and confused heart.

The huge figure of the incredible hulk came to mind, there was definitely anger in those green eyes, not mild irritation that is an emotion that can afford most domestic cats. But real untamed burning rage! There seemed to be a tiny flicker of a flame dancing in the depths of the darkness set there.

Bloody hell boyo, what was it that guy used to say, just before he burst into the unstoppable beast? "Don't make me angry, you won't like me when I'm angry!"

"No Stephen Fry for me then is that it, Buddy? No problem I don't like that show much anyhow!" The TV flickered and flashed as it died leaving the red dot in the corner staring down at him.

Immediately *The Cat* purred its acceptance, returning to his lap, placing its chin on its paws once more. The deep resounding purr that sounded more like the hum of a petrol generator than that of a domestic cat.

"We are gonna have to have a little chat sometime about manners and just who calls the shots here, Buddy!"

He had no intention of having that conversation. He already knew that there was something not right going on with this new friendship. But there remained always that sweet tart getting ever bigger pushing the savouries out of sight. That feeling one can never shroud from view, flattery, that feeling of being needed, cared for. We all strive for this, and sometimes it comes from the most unexpected places.

The Cat, reared its head back upwards, the skin of its throat vibrating with the strength of its purr. Green eyes, never blinking, gazing into his.

"What you wanna do then, Buddy? Go for drink, go to the movies, have an extra thick pizza with cheesy crust and regret it later?"

For once the eyes blinked, ever so slightly but a blink none the less.

"I guess not then. Probably a bad idea anyway."

Rick reached behind the wicker legs of the sofa, bringing out a beer at random from the box he had hidden underneath, using white teeth he bit the metal cap from it neck, spitting it across the tiled floor, the scraping noise pinched at the ears of *The Cat*.

"Bottoms up, Buddy!"

He drank, big thirsty gulps, the cold liquid couldn't leave the glass bottle fast enough for this thirst. He hadn't realised just how thirsty for it he was.

The rain outside had stopped, relinquishing its downpour only minutes after he had finished planting his new headstone.

He had changed his wet t-shirt and the fresh material felt soft against his wet skin. The beer finished, he placed it out of reach and grabbed another bottle. The cup of tea sat steaming on the sill, now long-forgotten.

His mind then turned to the little brunette he had been dealing with at the garden centre, she had become curious with this man, this doctor that had certainly become a welcome sight with his winning grin and interest in flowers and plants!

She had asked him, "May I ask, have you just moved or something? You could always purchase the plants and roses at once, I could always manage a little something off the price, well for you, anyway."

There had been, Rick knew, a hidden meaning there, as her pale cheeks had blossomed with a rosy pink, he was sure none of her soil-bound friends could never have compared with.

"No no, nothing like that at all, I just, I just...

AT this he had wavered slightly lost at what he would say to the question.

Oh no. Moved? Not at all, I seem to have this problem with other people's pets, they turn up on my lawn with their insides scattered all over the shop! It makes for one hell of a mess, so I bury them without telling anyone and plant the roses you sell me over them, you know, living headstone! Don't ask me why.

No, somehow he didn't think that would have been a very good response, instead he just smiled that winning grin that said, 'Hey trust me, I'm a doctor,' and continued, "I just had this, this idea that things, that things needed to change, you know things tend to get you down, when they stay the same. They can make you feel a little crazy. You know what I mean?"

"Oh, oh yeah, no problem!"

The cheeks had gone from the pinkie blush to pale as the grave, he had gotten the feeling she had no idea what he was trying to say!

The new bottle cap skipped across the tiles like a stone across a lake's surface, he drank. He drank heartily. The alcohol was a lit match placed by the edge of a dry pile of straw. The smoke was starting to burn strongly.

"Nice legs though, did you notice?"

The Cat just pawed his lap, hard enough to draw blood. Rick didn't notice, the smoke was turning into a flickering flame.

"Course not, you weren't there, nice though, very nice...

He drank, tapping his free fingers on the wicker arm chair, stillness encroached about him, it was times like this, when the pile of straw started to burn that he felt stronger, the flames and smoking giving power to his otherwise-dying engine.

Then out of the blue, he spoke, clear and strong, with such ferocity that *The Cat* stopped purring for a moment, ears shot backwards with surprise, then settling itself-back the way it was when it realised there was nothing to fear.

"It wasn't my fault! You know that's right, you hear what I'm saying, don't you, Buddy? It was not my fault."

He emptied the bottle with three long, harsh pain-inducing gulps that burned his throat. Tossing the bottle away, not caring where it landed, he reached for another, the metal cap pinging across the floor with fierce speed, bouncing of the wall opposite. He drank. He drank hard, the flames were really tearing at the straw now.

"It wasn't my fault, you know that I know that... but there are those who don't. Oh no, I'm not making it up. There are those who think I killed her, damn it! Killed her like some filthy murderer!

He drank, the liquid not slipping down the neck nearly as fast as he would have liked.

"Nosey, nosey, interfering bastards! That's who! People think I was on the booze, that's what they think. Well I wasn't. It was just a bad night. I checked, didn't I? There were three crashes on that stretch of motorway that night, three!"

Yeah, but no one died in the other two, did they boyo, no they didn't, only the one with your wife in the passenger seat that's the only one!

"It was raining, like it was earlier when I planted the headstone! And let's not forget old Natasha. Never liked driving at night."

No, please baby look how wet and dark it is, and you can bet they have turned the lamps off, you know how scared I get!"

Well, look at what bloody happened!

The beer bottle rolled away from his seat spilling some undrunk dregs on the tiles. *The Cat* looked up as though to make for it, but lowered its head and continued to paw his legs, purr and listen.

A bottle cap hit the glass door opposite.

"Well, damn it. See what happened! It was an accident, that's all, a goddamn accident!

Tears challenged him, he let them win.

"I couldn't see... just rain... wind... no lamps on..."

He sniffed violently, his shoulders rearing backwards with the force, he drank again. The straw was now a smouldering fire waiting to spread.

"But there are those who will argue that. Oh yes, you bet your white-furred arse on that. There are plenty of them. They think it was me, they think I was three sheets to the wind."

"Who?"

The word raked at the inside walls of his ears, those fingers of fear pressing at his temples, not quite as strong as they had been the first time, but the strength of the burning straw had numbed a little of that fear. It had seemed to be voiced by some soul deep in tone yet listless, a butterfly in a storm.

"Him next door!" Rick responded, without even thinking about it. When the fire's burning, it doesn't matter who is listening.

"Yeah him, he has always blamed me. He thinks it, I know he does. He has always hated me. Yeah, and he drinks more than I do, damn it. The bastard! And not this piss, the real stuff!"

He finished the beer. Another Bottle cap.

"He used to say things afterwards, never anything solid, he didn't have the balls for that, no chance. But he said things."

"What did he say, Richard?"

"He said once, '*Well, how awful, what a shame. You must miss her dreadfully. But you know, Rick if you play with a sprinkler, well sometime or another you're going to get wet*' What the hell does that mean, anyway?"

Rick gulped with big hearty gulps; the fire had consumed the straw and had turned its attention to anything that could burn! *The Cat* had stopped purring, its green eyes open, ears perked up erect.

The Cat was listening!

"Then there was the time I caught him talking to that sissy jogger, whatever his name is. They looked over at me when I got out the car, just cus they heard the bottle clink in the bags. Nosey bastards!"

Tears and snot mixed with the lager, giving it a bitter taste. He rubbed it away with the back of his hand, then wiped it across the side of his jeans.

"Oh, I know he thinks it, but I wasn't... I wasn't..."

He gulped again.

"Just one beer I had had, just one, oh that fat bastard next door, he really gets me worked up, that grin of his, if only he just disappeared, went away. It's his fault, this guilt, it must be. I have no other reason for feeling it, it's him; he makes me guilty, his eyes on me, his knowing! I hate him, if he just upped sticks and left, then it would go I'm sure of it, this guilt would go. That's why I drink, you know, it's the guilt, cus of him!"

This outpour continued for some time, tears, beer and burning straw, clouding all reason with its smoke. Rick had forgotten all about Rinty the dog. Casper the eighteen pound carp, he had forgotten picking the wet bloody clumps of wet fur from the thorns of the headstones, forgotten his pity for his neighbour.

The memory of Rinty's body, shredded like wood through a chipper, swollen on the water-clogged, rain-covered lawn. Those memories were gone now, the fire had driven them out, and It was unlikely they would ever crawl back up the back of his memory.

He sat drinking beer, ranting, with *The Cat* on his lap, who listened, green eyes never blinking, tail flicking.

★ ★ ★

People often underestimate the power of grief. It has this rather nasty habit of wrapping its knobbly talons around a person without much in the way of warning.

The hair of Sabena Jackson didn't hang with its usual air of self-confidence, nor did her make-up-free eyes, puffed with large bags under them, help her already-pitiful look.

She was rather unrecognisable. Standing in the doorway of her friend, Lizzie from work. Well she wasn't her friend, but Sabena had the tendency to use her plain 'friend' when the need arose, like when she needed a less attractive person to join her on night out, or when she needed Rinty walking and she just didn't have the time.

A shaking, yet well-manicured, finger pressed the doorbell for a tenth time, the buzzing rattling her already-strung-out nerves. The dream had scared her. She had not been able to forget the eyes. The green serpentine eyes that had loomed out from the darkened window.

Even so, standing there, waiting for the silent, sage-green door to open, she knew it was not the dream from which she usually suffered, the dream that had haunted her nights for years, the dream that held that voice, the voice in the background that seemed to reverberate through her heart and scream for her safety.

This dream had been different, but worse at the same time, there had never been a dream like it before, nothing close, it had been so real. She could still feel the coarseness in her throat form the thirst she had felt as Rinty.

The niggling little thought that, perhaps, wrapped up in herself she had maybe neglected that little pink dog, but the thought was turned away, she had enough to worry about.

She had to speak to someone. The doorbell rang again. No one answered.

Sabena stared at the door's light green, wooden frame, the square cut grooves that were cut out into it in parallel lines to the glass window that sat in the door's top. She willed the door to open. To hear the footfall of Lizzie, as she came trotting in her happy manner towards her, over the soft carpet Sabena knew to be behind the closed door.

Sabena had to speak to someone. Rinty was gone! Stolen during the night! Taken from right under her own small button nose. Had she really dreamt? Could it have been she had seen whoever it was that had taken him, without knowing it, some half-dream state, where reality meets the subconscious.

She dare not go back to the house. After frantically searching every room she had to come to the sad conclusion that Rinty, her only companion in the world, had been taken by some evil spiteful maniac.

The doorbell rang out loud again, longer this time, one droning tone. The curtains of Lizzie's neighbour twitched slightly.

Look. Go on, have a good bloody look. I don't care, let the whole bloody street look if it makes them happy!

Her thoughts were strung out, stressed and grey.

I Need. To. Speak. To. Someone. Anyone!!

No movement came from behind the green door.

What if it hadn't been Rinty that they were after? What if they were sending a message?

There she had said it, maybe not out loud, but she had said it none-the-less. The one thing she had been desperately trying to keep locked away in the treasury of unwanted ideas.

What if Rinty was just a warning, some sicko's idea of a joke, letting me know how close they had gotten, how close they had been to me!

The doorbell sang some rock'n'roll tune. The neighbour's curtains more than just twitched.

Look what I can take from your bedroom, look what I can do and you never even knew it. If I can do it again, do I get a prize?

Rinty had been her only friend. The only source of comfort to her lonely life, her family were never thought of. Well there was only her mother anyway after... after what had happened and they hated each other.

No regrets. Pure burning hatred from both sides. No score draw, everyone is a winner. Or loser. depending on how you looked at it.

It had been raining earlier, her hair frizzled with its effort to dry.

The neighbours watched as the rather dishevelled figure that kept ringing on the doorbell next door, hung her head and cried. The neighbours watched as whoever it was slumped down to her knees, and cried. She didn't go to help the young lady, there had always been a rather unhealthy snobbery in the Weepings: you can look, oh now that's just fine, but you don't touch.

No sir!

Meanwhile Lizzie Chambers had just finished her shopping at the local garden centre, where she had bumped into a very good looking, if slightly wet and dirty man who had smiled at her approvingly. She had been sure that at one time there had been some rather inappropriate gossip regarding this man, something to do with him being drunk and killing his wife in a car accident. But then Lizzie had always been the kind-hearted type that never gave much credence to gossip.

★ ★ ★

Night had drawn in, touching the light with its inky black, chilling the summer air with its contempt.

Dennis sat in his garage. The brick building, that had never been used to store his car, was not unlike the rest of his home. Spotless, one hundred Sherlocks with magnifying glasses before their eyes would not have found even the slightest hint of dirt. The room was spacious and well-ordered, shelves covered the walls with neatly arranged tools that he had never found the time to use. Most were still in their boxes.

The floor had rubber matting fitted throughout, like some super-scale jigsaw. An eighty-watt light bulb shaded by a plain blue plastic disco ball, hung from the centre of the ceiling.

He was sitting on his workshop stool, surrounded by the tools he had never even touched, relics from a past life before the seed of depression had grown into that glorious weed sucking the soil of his heart dry.

A man of method. A man of figures.

On the workbench a stereo system played the radio, the Scissor Sisters' song *Filthy/Gorgeous* strummed the otherwise-still atmosphere.

He sipped Jim Beam, the strong liquid slipping down his throat unhindered with shame or regret at his drunken state and situation.

No son of a bitch gonna treat me like a ho!

His bare left foot tapped along with the beat, hot and sweaty with the feel of the rubber on his dry skin. He snatched a look at the time on his wristwatch: 01:30am

He drank from the glass, the light was very bright and he was very drunk. He tried hard to think, to follow a steady train of thought, the condition he was in, this was no easy feat.

You're so filthy, and I'm gorgeous!

His head lolling from side to side, eyes half closed, Dennis felt rather happy. He had finally plucked up the courage after all this time, all these years of hatred and bitter, twisted worms of despair crawling around in his gut. No more excuse. This would show them all!

He drained the glass and placed it out of reach, it was his last ever drink.

There hung from one long wooden rafter in the ceiling a noose, a simple homemade affair.

You Make Me Feel So Nasty!

He stood on vein-blistered legs, the world about him was very heavy at the moment. Fat sausages fumbled with the plastic stool, somewhere deep in the part of his mind that hadn't been totally taken over by the weed, had thought, *I hope this thing takes my weight!*

He laughed a drunken laugh that if anyone else had heard would have sounded more like a small sob of indignation. He struggled onto the plastic frame. It groaned and bent slightly, but it held. Just! He pulled the noose over his head, the rope tickled his neck.

Tina Turner took over the vocal race late at night.

Life time of promises, world of dreams

Dennis sobered up, he could see his mother and father...

Speak the language of love like you know what it means!

They were smiling at him...

Ummm it can't be wrong!

Now he was in college, the only man he had ever loved standing before him toned and strong, Billy. He had been the only person he had ever let beat him at squash!

Take my heart and make it strong!

Now he was seeing his father again, bald head and small squinting eyes peering at him with the mark of distaste etched into the lines that framed them. He was shouting at him, those small eyes had not been thought of for a long, long time.

You're simply the best!

Dennis fell. Whether he had kicked aside the plastic chair or if he had slipped in the last seconds of his life was never known for sure.

Had Dennis not had the radio on... Had Dennis not been so drunk... Had he not been so wrapped up times gone by... he might have seen a pair of green eyes staring at him in the darkness, as he placed the noose over his head.

But he hadn't noticed. And he was not found for two days, not until his colleagues at Baker Works who had never really understood him, became concerned for the best accountant they had ever had.

Morning brought with it a sense of calm. Rick woke with a start; his head hurt once again, his eyes were black holes on the face of the moon.

Coughing out his sleepy tiredness, he blinked moronically, looking about him.

"I've slept here all night?"

This question needed no answer.

He was still slumped in the sofa of the conservatory, feet spread out before him, empty bottles lay about his feet, the air smelt like stale beer and made his headache worse. He stifled a deep surging movement in his stomach.

There was no cat.

This had registered more meaning to him than it might have done to anyone else within the same situation. Sobering fast he stood, the room swaying slightly as he did so.

There was that churning deep down in the stomach again. A washing machine on turbo, last night's beer mixed with anxious, fear-fuelled adrenaline.

The Cat's not here! Christ, The Cat's not here!

His mind raced with fresh horrors. It felt as though there were a thousand spiders crawling about under his t-shirt. His skin leaked alcohol-tainted sweat.

Tentatively he leant his forearm against the sliding door, and looked into the garden.

The Cat, sitting upright with the sun on its back, tail flicking behind its back, sitting looking, looking down, across the distance between them, swallowed up by the magnitude of what Rick could see placed in the centre of the lawn.

"You're welcome!"

There passed a few seconds.

Then Rick's turbo spin jumped and lurched. The remains of last night's work splattered across the patio.

★ ★ ★

There passed many incidents over the two days that Dennis hung like a chicken in his garage, his lips turning blue. When he was found, the police were called in. They arrived just before it had turned dark. They spent a lot of time in the garage, this was no usual suicide. But suicide they were sure it was.

Detective Inspector Rowlings had stayed on in the lonely building that had served as Dennis's tomb, after the team had left and moved on into the main house. The scene was not all that different than the many others that she had dealt with.

DI Rowlings stood, her arms folded across her chest, weight resting on one foot. The search for a suicide note proceeded in the main house.

She didn't expect to find one. This sort very rarely did. No one to write to.

Her practical and seasoned mind was well-suited for this sort of job. Her attention once again turned to the dried and mottled stain of blood that had left a circle on the rubber mats that had made up the flooring.

To the empty garage she muttered, "This is new, this is not right."

It was suicide. Pure and simple, yet one that she would not forget for some time. Her young sergeant interrupted her meanderings.

"Ma'am, we have searched the main house, nothing to report. Just very clean and tidy in there, everything is spotless, made me regret the mess we made a bit."

"Thank you, sergeant."

She knew exactly what he was thinking. The suicide victim had been homosexual, repressed no doubt, there had been no mirrors or photographs of family or friends in the house. Not proof of course, but it was enough to bring a small amount of pity to the inspector's calm demeanour.

She asked, "Any luck with the neighbours?"

"There is only one to speak of, right next door, being a cul-de-sac and all. A doctor of some sort, I don't know, though seemed as though he hasn't worked for some time, we are doing a check on him. He was gardening when I called. Couldn't help much, said that Mr Pye was a quiet man who kept himself to himself, said and I quote...

With this, the young police officer flicked open a small black notebook and read from its pages, "'Dennis was always very polite and respectful, I couldn't have asked for a better neighbour, I shall miss him and the sound of his pond!' That was all he had to say."

The notebook snapped shut and found the sergeant' back pocket. The two police officers had stood looking at one another, with a quiet understanding.

Finally, the inspector took the initiative.

"Any sign at all of his foot?"

The sergeant had been waiting with his reply.

"No ma'am, afraid not. Mighty strange though, the doc says it had been, well, torn and ripped as if some animal had bitten it off! There are no blood stains once you get passed the garage's back door, which was shut!"

The inspector nodded her understanding and with a quick movement of her eyes she let her young officer know that was all; he was dismissed.

The body of Dennis Pye had been found hanging from the neck, the home made noose holding strong. His left foot missing, cut and ripped violently halfway below the knee, shin bone resembling wood splinters had guided the flow of blood onto the waiting rubber mats.

His body had been taken to the hospital, where nobody enquired about him. As far as anyone knows he was buried by the Co-op and there was only Mr Charles Boston in attendance. He would, if forced, have admitted he would have rather been playing golf.

★ ★ ★

After finding the foot, Rick had been sick, collected himself together, and been sick again.

Now he was driving, and driving fast! He was on a motorway to somewhere, he wasn't sure where.

After he had been sick he had stood for a long time, minutes had become hours for him, the walls of the conservatory might just have been a blur, unrecognisable moments in time. Believe it or not though, he had felt better after the digested beer had made its exit.

Cleared the tubes. As they say.

He had buried the foot in the same way as he had Casper the friendly carp, and Rinty the pink poodle. There had never really been any doubt that he would. He hadn't got a gravestone yet, but all in due course.

After sliding the door open he had walked straight to the shed, daring not to look down on the irregular gift. A trance had seemed to engulf him, everything, his breathing, walking, taking up the shovel had been done in automatic.

Like he was driving now, everything done in the third person. He had an image of a tractor running, ploughing the earth, but the driver, some comical figure with a flat cap, braces and a piece of straw in the corner of his mouth, facing backwards, feet up on the fender, reading a paper.

He drove faster.

He started to think, to try desperately to calm his mind, to turn that farmer around and take control.

It couldn't have been a coincidence. No, it was *The Cat*, it had to be. But that was impossible.

Never heard of anything like this happening before! But it's got to be a coincidence!

He remembered the drunken conversation with *The Cat* the night before, the way he had droned on about his hatred for Dennis, placing the blame for everything at his feet.

Well, his foot! Ha!

He drove faster.

Had *The Cat* really understood what he had been saying? He seemed to have done, Rick had noticed, not for the first time just how contented *The Cat* would sit and listen. The perfect counsellor.

Had *The Cat* killed him?

Don't be stupid, he is man of over 15 stone, not some bitch's pink poodle out for a walk!

He thought about the way the bone had poked up from under the folded, fat skin.

Peak-a-boo!

He drove faster.

He knew it had to be Dennis's foot. It was the fattest foot he had ever seen. The bone poking out jumped behind his eyes once again, a white mole digging its way to the top of red earth, come to say hello.

He laughed, his stomach churned. He controlled it. Continued to think.

Dennis must be dead! Has to be. The cat couldn't kill him for Christ's sake, think about it for a second it is just a cat! The man must be dead! Choked himself on a cake, or some super-sized bag of crisps.

That made him smile. He slowed the speed of the car. Yes it made sense to him. Dennis had died and *The Cat* had found him.

Maybe he had even cut the foot off by accident. Yes, that's it, he cut his foot off with some power tool. Then the cat found him dying and spluttering. That's perfect!

He knew there was no chance of this; in the years he had known Dennis he had never known him to do any DIY for himself, he was the kind of guy that always hired in. Hands soft as pastry.

The car sped up once more.

Then slowed, a van in the fast lane doing sixty-five, he undertook it, moved back over, and watched his speedometer twitch up to a hundred miles an hour.

This cat! He knew it was *The Cat*. Something deep down inside himself - the part that always knew that he had a drink problem but never spoke out loud, the part that knew Natasha had once had a fling with an old college friend but that he had never mentioned to her -

that part of him knew that there was something terribly wrong with this cat, the part that knew he should have stopped it a long time ago!

Thinking about Natasha seemed to punch the speedometer ever further along its dial.

What would Natasha say? What would she do? Another slow driver, he undertook, his brakes squealing, returned back to the fast lane, the long-past motorist's horn resounding about in the motorway's polluted air. Rick didn't hear it.

I'll ring the cats' home. I'll ring them, tell them it's not working. They can have him back!

He placed the right thumb and forefinger against his forehead, rubbing the tight skin there; the feeling made him somehow more awake.

He didn't want to believe that *The Cat* had, could have, killed Dennis.

The guy's foot is buried three feet deep in your garden, boyo, he didn't bloody donate it now, did he!

Now, what really bothered Rick, what really flicked at the gonads of his self control, was not the memory of the dead fish, the sodden fur of the dead dog or the fat foot without a leg.

It was that cream-filled tart that just seemed to be about the only real feeling left. All the others, disgust, fear, repulsion, they had become a sort of act. Some Oscar-winning performance. He knew full well he had no intention of giving back *The Cat*. All he needed was to get that lazy farmer back facing the right way again!

He was flattered! He liked the attention. He was detached from reality.

The creamy tart is always there, even if you don't lean forward and take a bite, it's always there!

He slowed the car.

Don't want to be pulled over now, do you? No way, boyo, that would just give everyone something else to tittle-tattle about. Nosey bastards!

"I'll keep him locked in. Yes, that's what I'll do, keep the furry nightmare locked in the house!"

Problem solved.

He was feeling better. Sherlock had solved the case. Keep *The Cat* locked in. The answer had been screaming at him all along. Just keep it locked inside.

He switched the radio on. Lionel Richie was dancing on the ceiling. Rick tapped his fingers on the steering wheel. The car now well within the speed limit.

What is happening here?

The farmer seemed to be back facing the right way again.

Room is hot uhh and that's good!!

Rick drove, contented with the decision he had made. *The Cat* was not to blame. *The Cat* was good. *The*

Cat's eyes were green and they reminded him of Natasha.

The Cat was good!

When he got home, he pulled onto the driveway. *The Cat* was sitting on the windowsill, watching as he pulled quietly up, seemingly almost not wanting to wake some unseen evil entity.

He didn't look up at Dennis's bungalow as he turned his key in his lock.

The Cat greeted him. There was enough light left in the day for him to clean up the sick and spilt beer, stomach churning once again. He made a promise to himself not to drink again that night.

After dark, Rick donned his black training tracksuit, not that it got much use these days and gloves, which reminded him suddenly of a patient he once had, who had always worn black gloves.

He scaled the fence, jumping into Dennis's garden. He used a torch to shed light on the otherwise-dark property.

The garage door had a light on though, spitting its light out in rays.

He looked inside and saw the dead body of his neighbour hanging from the ceiling. His foot removed, the blood had stopped dripping sometime before.

Rick got into bed, stroked *The Cat* and had a dreamless sleep. The next day he would buy a Boxwood plant shaped like a dog with a stick in its mouth. Whilst planting it, he would be questioned by a young police officer. And Rick would smile and lie through his back teeth!!

* * *

From then on Rick kept *The Cat* indoors. He had received little-to-no resistance from *The Cat* to this, which had greatly surprised him.

Two weeks had passed since the foot had arrived on his lawn. He was drinking less and he felt as though those few days were just a bad dream that would disappear as all nightmarish memories will, so long as you allow yourself to move on.

The first thing he had done was to block up the cat flap with ply board. Thick as his thumbnail. *The Cat* had shown not the slightest interest in this. Rick's t-shirt had stuck to his back with perspiration. *The Cat* had just sat motionless watching him eyes half-hidden by long-lashed lids of indifference.

Rick was also enjoying his new interest in gardening; the roses were certainly flourishing, as well the evergreen bushes he had placed in the make-shift cemetery.

Must be the rich nutrients buried beneath them.

He had smiled dryly to this idea. The thing is, he was probably right; nothing works better than a good scattering of bone meal to bring out the best in flowering plants.

He was happy. Not only had the farmer turned to face the right way, he had lost forty pounds and was now singing a happy tune!

Then the letter arrived, no post mark or return address.

HELLO DR COOPER,

I KNOW YOU DR COOPER, I KNOW WHAT YOU DID. OR SHOULD I SAY MR COOPER. NOT BEEN TO WORK FOR A WHILE NOW, HAVE WE? I KNOW YOU! I KNOW WHAT YOU DID, I KNOW YOU WERE DRUNK. YOU WERE DRUNK AND YOU KILLED YOUR WIFE! YOU'RE NOT FIT TO BREATHE THE SAME AIR AS THE REST OF US GOOD PEOPLE. A DIRTY DRUNK. WE ALL KNOW. AND DON'T THINK YOU CAN GET AWAY WITH IT! OR ANYTHING ELSE THAT YOU HAVE DONE! YOU'RE ALL WRONG!

FROM AN ENEMY!

That was it! The plug had been pulled right there and then. The tank that controlled his backed-up memories set free to flow as it pleased, soaking that fat farmer who was not even sitting in the seat now but laying over it with his arse in the air.

It all flooded back to him. Everything that he knew but had somehow managed to suppress.

They had been to a party. Her friend's party. The old colleague that he and Natasha never spoke of had not been there; he had been secretly glad about that. He had promised not to drink. But he had.

Old Ahab gotta chase that whale!

She hadn't protested. She was used to it, besides he had always been able to hide it well. The weather was bad, it was raining.

Had it been rain or sleet?

Of course it wasn't sleet; it had been the first week in September, nearly a year ago to the day.

She had been snoozing, sleeping. It hadn't been a long drive; he had done much further before. Much further and much more drunk, that's for sure.

There had been a lot of traffic.

Now, he let himself slump back into his sofa, the letter crunched in his fist, trying to squeeze the life out of whoever had sent it.

I was lucky, that was all, just lucky. If you can call it that.

He laughed. He reached behind him, searching for a beer. He found one and bit the bottle top from its neck!

AH there is a new bartender in town, Sofa Wickes, the beer's always warm, but he just never seems to run out.

He laughed once more. He drank from the bottle. Savouring the wet taste, ignoring its tepid temperature. He looked over to the living room entrance, there sat *The Cat*. Their eyes met. The green depths there seemed to swallow him up, he could see nothing else, they grew there before him, a sleepy dream seized him, pulling him by the belt.

He was there, he could see it all, the car on its roof, all the windows smashed and shattered, sharp edges left jutting out of their frames like sharks' teeth.

The lights blazing from the headlights, rain bouncing on the floor, creating intermittent shadows all around him.

The sound of sirens, the flashing red lights.

And Natasha, lying fifteen feet from the car. Her head had looked slightly better than the remains of Rinty, but not by much.

He had lost control, hit a bollard on the hard shoulder, she had no seatbelt on. She hadn't died when her 39-year-old head turned to mincemeat through the windscreen. She had somehow survived the crash.

She had taken the seatbelt off to be more comfortable to sleep.

He had done everything right, he was a doctor! When the ambulance came - he could see it so clearly, he was standing before it all - he had taken control. She was his wife, after all. He was well-known and respected. Well-known in his profession to be one year from consultancy.

And he had been drunk. He had driven her drunk, seat belt off so she could sleep better for it.

No one had asked the question.

They didn't ask, even then, with your wife dying, you were feeling, feeling… relived. Weren't you? Yes, you were relieved!

The police hadn't even asked the question, he had been too damn good at taking control. He had had to make a statement.

He was there now, watching himself, like some nosey parker watching some distasteful moment in a stranger's life.

He remembered calculating time, time from when he had last drunk, from when the ambulance had arrived, when they had got back to the emergency room.

He cried, as he was pulled once again by the belt, pulled back in time to his rotten memories, vivid and real. He remembered telling the staff he needed time to be alone, told the police to give him some time to settle and calm before the statement was made.

Yeah, you needed time alright. You needed time to get that secret stash of toothpaste and toothbrush from your desk didn't you! Didn't you!

He cried and trembled in the wicker chair as he remembered more vividly than he had ever seen anything in his whole life, the way he had brushed, the door locked to his office. Oh he had brushed. He had brushed and brushed. His wife had been dead for minutes and he brushed his teeth. He could see the office clock on the wall, the second hand dragging slowly about its face; he brushed and brushed, calculating time in his head. He was a clever man, Richard Cooper.

He remembered the way his tears had worked into his mouth watering the minty toothpaste; it had run down his sleeve! The taste filled his mouth again where he sat in his conservatory

Then, sitting there on his sofa, he dropped the beer bottle from his hand. He had blacked out. The onset of memories and their meaning had downed the farmer in his field.

He woke, finding himself on the cold floor, the beer bottle rolled away under the sofa. *The Cat* sat inches from him. His vision was full of green diamonds.

He washed, shaved and changed his clothes. The letter he had torn and burnt using the matches that Natasha had used to smoke with. Funny, he hadn't even thought about smoking since Natasha had died.

Don't want to have to smell them on those teeth, boyo, might have to brush and brush and brush and brush!

He now sat in the lounge. *The Cat* on his lap, purring its concern at him, the tail flicked behind its head. Rick felt calmer once more. He had just needed to let the waters flow, to let the plug out.

A ship battered after a long storm. He floated on calm seas.

Besides, he knew who had sent the letter. Sabena was responsible. He knew it almost at once, the way the letter had been written, so childish and repetitive.

Don't think you can get away with it, or anything else you have done! Anything else you have done! From an enemy!

So simple. She was blaming him for the loss of her dog. She hated him. They all hated him. He was sure of that.

He stroked *The Cat*'s ears.

"Wish I had killed the little shit!"

He looked down into the purring cat's eyes, never blinking.

"Never mind, you took care of that little job, didn't you!"

He sipped at the top of a new beer. This one was cold; it had come from the fridge, much better thank you!

The perfume, Sabena you silly cow!

The letter had smelled so strongly of scent that it had burnt quicker than any paper should. The smell had brought to mind that colour of pink that he always had when around her.

"Stupid, stupid shit!"

The fact that Rick had figured out who had sent the letter lifted his spirits remarkably. An evil balloon had popped before it had ever been allowed to take to the air.

It had been Sabena. For a short while he had been niggled by the idea that it might have been one of his doctor colleagues. The ones that had suggested that he take some well needed, "Requested long leave".

He had always known that they knew. But they wouldn't say anything. He was a free man. But he wasn't allowed to work.

It had definitely been Sabena. Nothing to worry about there; after all, she was nothing to him.

Just some crazy blonde tart, buddy, she ain't nothing to us, let her talk and send her nasty letters, I don't care about it!

At about two o'clock that night, *The Cat* jumped down from Rick's lap. After taking one long look at him still sat in the lounge chair, it quickly drifted off towards the blocked cat flap. There followed a crisp, cracking, splintering of wood that cracked into the darkness like a whip.

Then, once again, after the cat flap swung down shut, there was only silence.

★ ★ ★

Sabena removed the make-up from her face with military precision. Sabena had enjoyed her night out, the first time she had really enjoyed herself since she had lost Rinty.

Stilettos and cigarettes.

The 'pink' smelling perfume clambered about her like a flowery haze.

She stood up, placing the pink make-up stool under the dressing table. Standing before her mirrored wardrobe doors she let the thin dress she always wore when dancing, drop to her ankles.

Her bra and panties, a delicious shade of red. Sabena cut a fine figure. She knew it, too. Leaning forward, eyeing her reflection, her lips sucked together in a pout as she thought about her actions earlier that day.

After Rinty had first disappeared, the fear of another visit from the dognapper - pointed nose, top hat, and whip - had plagued her repeatedly. A feeling that she couldn't shake off, a feeling of being unclean, of not being safe, that one night she could wake to see the figure, top hat and pointed nose, grinning down at her, repulsive wart twitching with pleasure.

Lizzie had found her that day, when she had so badly needed to talk to someone, found her crying on her doorstep. Being a good friend she had let Sabena stay with her for a time. But it hadn't suited Sabena's life style. She had always liked to be in control. Make the decisions of her life, and rooming with the friendly, but rather frumpy, work colleague had not been at all suitable. She had quickly lost patience with the need to be on her own, the initial fear subsiding with time.

Her reflection looked sensual, her long, tanned legs tight together and partially bent at the knees. She let her long hair down, it encased her well-shaped face in a golden frilly frame. Her red lips snapped together as she blew herself a kiss.

Her vanity, sometimes it knew no bounds, especially when she was feeling proud of herself and, today, remembering the letter she had posted through the door of the evil doctor, the dognapper, she happened to be boiling over her pretty top with pride.

She stretched her limbs, the muscles within aching from the busy night of dancing. Sabena didn't drink, she never had done, but she liked the attentions of those who did, as she moved her body about the dance floor. Tonight had been no different.

Sitting down on her bed, arms out behind her, her head hanging back behind her, hair golden and perfectly straight, she lay on the soft duvet. The memory of how the penny had dropped.

Clink! Just like that. It had come to her that sudden. It was the doctor. Trying to scare her, to remind her that she had once turned him down. That he was capable of anything, even taking her pet dog.

It had been the drunk doctor. She should have known sooner. The idea of going to the police had crossed her mind. But, as always with Sabena, her decision was made and without much debate.

I cooked his goose! Good and proper, ha ha! This cat has claws!

After her breaking piece of detective work, Sabena had moved right back home. The fact that it was him, the drunken doctor that everyone knew had killed his wife, it had annoyed her. She was no longer afraid. There had been no need to be afraid in the first place, he was nothing to be afraid of.

I bet he still has Rinty, anyway, over there in that house of his. All tied up. Well, I will get him back, I will teach the doctor what it means to upset this pussy cat!

She stood, hands on hips, lips twisted into a smirk that rather stole her good looks and made her a trifle ugly, a rare occurrence for Sabena.

The letter had felt good. It had felt satisfying to write and it had felt even better as she had posted it through his door.

She had just walked right up and slipped it through the letterbox, no problem. She hadn't cared if she had been seen or even if he had seen her for that matter. This kitten was on a high, claws out ready to scratch.

She had not cared much if he had guessed it was her sending the love letter either, spraying it wither most expensive perfume.

The closest he's ever gonna get to sniffing that up close!

Giggling, she started to strut out of the bedroom, her body relishing the movement. Sabena was on fire, the idea that the letter might have stirred a little storm down the road excited her more than any drunken admirer.

Her bathroom was very feminine, like the rest of her house. In its centre there stood a free-standing bath, bronzed legs keeping its marble frame off the floor. Very nice. Very Hollywood.

Hot tap running, bubble bath floating its white bubbles into the air. Radio playing Bublé in the background. Scented candles lit. The place was the very picture of the Hollywood actress. The most beautiful babe in the Weepings; there was no doubt about it.

This was one hell of a wave called ego.

Unfortunately for the attractive blonde, she didn't notice *The Cat*. Not until she had slid her naked body, that any man would have told his darkest secrets to get a chance to see, into the warm water covering her shoulders, her head lifted out over the white bubbles. Hot steam rose in waves of smoky, sensual delight! Flickering with shadows made by the burning candles.

She gave a little start of alarm, her body jolting, legs raising, sending water out of the marble bath. *The Cat* was sitting in the bathroom's doorway. She couldn't make it out very clearly, it was just a black silhouette, the light from the bedroom beyond reaching down the corridor and sending the animal's shadow creeping about the bathroom's floor.

The flickering candles sent dancing shadows and dark whips of steam across its frame.

"Where the hell have you come from! Cat, where the hell are you from!"

Sabena hated cats, and she especially hated cats that attacked her Rinty or turned up in her bathroom, uninvited, late at night.

The Cat, more like a small lion in the moonlight, didn't make a move. Its ears flicked slightly in the darkened shadow of its archway.

There was a long silence. Then *The Cat* made a small noise. Very slight, the simplest of meows, a whisper of irritation.

I really hate cats! Where the hell have you come from?

Sabena giggled, her self-control returning. The shock was gone and left in its wake the feeling of indignation. How dare this filthy animal be in her wonderfully perfect home?

Sabena might not have known it, but the most beautiful girl in the town was in the most danger she had ever been in her life.

As she stared at *The Cat*, the smirk she had found on her face started to drip away. It looked an awful lot like that cat the doctor had. The one that had hurt poor Rinty! An uneasy feeling reared up from inside and tugged at her insides. There was something not right with this, the way it just sat there, she could see even in the light of the flickering candles that it was looking right towards her, never wavering in its stare.

"Go on now, scatt!"

She clapped her hands together, water jumped from her wet palms. *The Cat* yawned, a never-ending yawn that made Sabena feel very unsure as to what exactly was sitting before her and her escape. She had accepted fear into her heart once again.

Bang! The radio went out with a smoky, sparking snap. Smoke crept out of its speaker. Sabena knew it had been *The Cat*, *The Cat* had killed the radio.

Another unhappy feeling then seemed to replace the bath water slopping about her naked body, vulnerability.

The Cat's shadow arched its back, the hair raised, it flicked the tail behind its head, a tail too big, she thought to herself.

Cats don't have tails that big, they... they just don't look like this.

Green eyes burned through the darkness of its silhouette, two headlights on a train in a tunnel and Sabena could well have been the damsel tied to the tracks before it.

The shadowy shape of a cat before her started to change, to shift and stretch. Slowly it appeared to get larger still, its green eyes raging green fire that seemed to reach out to her across the bathroom.

Sabena's hands that had been gripping the cold marble went limp, flopping as if lifeless into the warm water. She started to open her mouth, perhaps to scream, but all the lungs beneath her fake, implanted breasts could muster was a pathetic whistle. Her skin turned white, her simple decisive mind unable to cope with what her eyes were relaying to it.

It was then that Sabena, 30 years old, unmarried and very unhappy, finally made sense of the old nightmares that had haunted her for years. Right that second before she died it all became clear as crystal. She could see it all again, it was Daddy who had been calling her name, she could see it now in the full scope of her terror, right before her, she could hear his voice crying out her name, and it was Daddy. Daddy, who used to buy her ice cream at the beach, daddy who used to tell her night-time stories, it was Daddy that had promised on his heart that real monsters didn't exist. Daddy who had died when she had swam out to far! Daddy who had cried for her and then cried even louder for himself! Daddy who had died when she had swam out too deep! Too deep for him to follow her!

Her face blackened out by the shadow before, told of terrors now far greater than anything she could see approaching her in the very feminine bathroom.

★ ★ ★

Rick awoke, his right elbow slipping off the edge of the lounge chair's arm-rest.

Had he been dreaming? He couldn't remember. The first thing that entered his sober brain:

I'm sober! Christ, I'm waking up and I'm sober!

Scrambling for the watch on his wrist he checked the time that read in blood-red digital, 03:00.

He rubbed his eyes, groggy mist clouded memories that he was reluctant to let slip back into his conscious mind.

Sometimes sleep really is the best medicine. Complete and non-interrupted! That's this doctor's prognosis, anyway.

The letter had made its way up that memory bank! He wished he hadn't woken, deciding to get into bed and hope he never woke.

He stood, intending to do just that, rubbing his aching legs.

Man, I am seriously getting out of shape!

Stretching his back that groaned and creaked under the pressure, he was unprepared for what was about to happen.

It hit him; never before had he felt anything like this. Pain mixed with a sickly desire to run, to run and never look back! Those fingers weren't just probing at his temples, they were kneading like a baker into his skull! He closed his eyes and threw his head back screaming in confused anger and pain, there seemed to be some unseen fingertips pawing at the insides of his ears.

And then he heard it.

The voice.

This time much clearer.

"Come and see me. Come and see me now Richard."

A voice, rattling about inside his deranged guilt-riddled head. He grabbed his ears trying to shake off unseen headphones. But there were none to be found. It was just a natural reaction to a very unnatural action.

It's alright, just try again, just try again. Just turn around and go to bed. It's one big nightmare. All nightmares end.

With that he started to panic that there was no cat. He couldn't see *The Cat*. He couldn't see it anywhere. He groped the walls trying desperately to find the light switch.

It came again. A full blown wave of intrusion.

"Come and see me. Come and see me on the lawn! I have something for you, something that I know you will cherish. Oh yes, Richard, this is the crown jewel. Come and see me. Come and see me!"

Rick stretched his eyes so wide they might have fallen out onto the carpet by his feet. Nails scratched so hard at his temples they drew beads of blood, reddening the dirt beneath his nails. His teeth clenched so tightly his jaw burned with the exertion.

This was too much for him. What terrors must he endure now? He stumbled into the conservatory.

Oh great show, boyo, the one time you wake up and you're not as drunk as a skunk, and you still can't walk in a straight line!

Holding his stomach with both hands as though he had been shot there, he turned to face the sliding door's glass window. He could see nothing, it was too dark. He would have to flick the garden's light switch.

Natasha then swam unhindered through his mind, the last of the toothpaste as he hid in his office, the image of that clock on the wall, second hand ticking ever slower, dragging itself along. He remembered thinking how much he would have given to just be able to grab that hand and turn it backwards, just keep turning and turning it until time itself might have turned back. To the time before... before he had killed Natasha. Before he had killed Natasha! But, of course, that was fantasy, and doctors don't believe in fantasy, so he had just stood there looking at the clock, frantically trying to brush away the taste and smell of beer. The spittle and mint running ever further down his arm and under his armpit, dripping onto his waistline. He remembered the looks, the knowing looks on his partner's face, the mixture of sympathy, pity and loathing. He tried to twist his mind from it, but it clawed back the toothpaste, the clock, the sirens.

Then the voice intruded this destructive marathon of self-hate.

"Rick! Come and see me. See what I have. See my loyalty, see my devotion to you and only you. It can only be me and you Rick, there is no room for the vermin that infect your life. Come and see me!"

As he turned his attention to the window once more he looked more like a man turning to see the spot where his car had been parked only to see a burning mass of molten plastic.

Holding on to his stomach, he swallowed hard.

That's right boyo, hold onto that stomach, wouldn't want to let go. Heaven forbid

Reaching with his left hand he placed shaking fingers on the switch for the garden light. He hesitated.

For just that second he hesitated!

"There can only be me and you. Come and see what I have, it's ever-so fragile and pretty, come and see me!"

He flicked the switch.

The car might well have been transported away by a UFO, for his face was beyond any felling a sane man has ever experienced.

The artificial light lit up the garden, roses and evergreens shrouded in light, lying behind a vision that fragmented Rick's brain into the very real state of insanity.

Sat in the middle of the lawn was *The Cat*. He knew it was *The Cat*, it had green eyes. But that was where the resemblance ended.

The creature was larger and blacker than any panther, yet slim in build. Wiry muscles, veined with blood, adorned the limbs, the face seemed more serpent than cat, flecked with scattered markings like a reptile's skin. Hundreds of sharp teeth protruded over the bottom lip, they were a snake's set of fangs. The green eyes were elongated like the most perfect diamonds, glinting with a feline-like, feverish delight. Ears of a bat, two feet high, rose from the side of its head. Its tail, a lion's tail, yet furless, flicked behind its head.

The fingers kneaded his temples once more, yet he didn't seem to notice the discomfort.

"Do you see, Rick? Do you see how much I care? do you see how it is to be free?"

Rick became aware then of the body, the wet, naked, blood-soaked and almost shrivelled body of Sabena! Limp and prostrate, facing up towards the black sky. The creature had one of its talon like claws buried deep in her side. Blood, dark and fresh, seeped about the muscled countenance. The claws suddenly tightened, the body shook, Sabena's dead body danced with blood.

"Come and see me!"

Rick didn't move. He couldn't. Even if he had wanted to. The only thought that he had was to flick the switch. Make the scene disappear. Make it go away.

If I can't see it, it can't be real. If I can't see it, it can't be real!

"Oh but it is, you don't understand yet, but you will, Rick. They always do. In the end they always see me. They learn to understand!"

The automatic pilot took control.

Please put your seat belts on, everyone, and put your head between your knees, there may be some turbulence ahead!

Rick slid open the door, bare feet on the damp grass. His toes enjoying the coolness of the grass.

It's the little things boyo, the little things!

He walked to the creature, *The Cat*. He didn't look at the naked body. He could smell the perfume. He didn't think of the colour pink.

"I, myself, cannot read. But I do not think that there will be any more letters. Do you?"

Rick was floating now. His senses heightened, the coolness of the night a friendly breeze rippling happily on his t-shirt.

The Cat released its grip on the body. A long, forked serpent's tongue licked at the blood on those bird-of-prey-like talons. Rick imagined some snake/cat hybrid.

He wanted to laugh, but couldn't. Then *The Cat* jumped behind itself, its tail flicking by Rick's ear. It jumped onto the shed roof, without so much as a sound. As quiet as a cat.

Rick thought of the shed's roof collapsing under its weight, saws, forks, and spades piercing its flesh and killing it.

The Cat, resting itself on its paws, serpent eyes green and never blinking, looked into Rick's soul. It looked right past his eyes and found his inner heart.

"You're welcome!"

The door of the shed opened. Rick's old automatic pilot taking over once more. He walked towards the shed. He didn't bother to ask himself how the shed's door had managed to open without help. It seemed to be the least of his worries.

He was floating in a world of dreams. Nightmares and blue smoke, blacks and purples of the world that couldn't exist!

As he walked under the shed's door way, he sneaked a peak up towards *The Cat* perched above. Had he not been floating, he may have screamed his lungs to dust, the eyes were leering right at him, its neck stretched down towards him, the green there taken on an evil meaning in torment and flame; the teeth, the hundreds of teeth were parted in a Cheshire Cat grin.

The moon hung behind its bat's ears, there was stale breath on its teeth.

"Not all dreams scatter with the sun, Richard! Sometimes nightmares remain."

At that moment, inches from the face of his own insanity, Rick felt that is was all so simple.

Why fight the tide? Boyo, it only ever flows faster. Until you lose your footing. You can't stop the world from turning.

And Natasha was dead.

Dead and buried.

There's an awful lot of vermin in the world, boyo!

★ ★ ★

The next morning Rick made black coffee, he stroked the white cat, its fur soft and spotlessly clean.

He took Natasha's cigarettes out from her dressing table.

Rick hadn't smoked since the party, the party the night Natasha had died.

But today he really wanted to smoke.

The sunshine had dried the dampness out of the earth. He stepped out onto the patio. *The Cat* ran out onto the lawn. It showed no interest in the mound of freshly-turned earth on its surface.

Rick placed his aviator sunglasses on his nose.

Maverick! This kid is cooler than McQueen!

He had buried the body of the most beautiful women he had ever met, deep. It hadn't taken him long, he had found strength he never knew he had or could possess.

He sipped the black coffee. The sun felt simply utopian!

He placed the cigarette between his teeth, he looked at *The Cat* on the shed's roof. Tenderness swamped him.

The cream-filled tart had been well-and-truly snapped up and eaten, and right now he was wiping its remains from satisfied lips.

He loved *The Cat*.

The Cat reminded him of Natasha!

The Cat was good!

The sulphur from the match stung at his nostrils. His toes curled around the warm blades of grass.

He breathed in the smoke.

Dr Jimmy Cobbs entered his mind's eye!

The cigarette burnt as he drew on its torched tobacco, inhaling deeply. Filling his lungs.

Natasha had loved the sunshine.

Jimmy Cobbs had been the main instigator in having Rick struck off.

And let's face it, he had been struck off.

Jimmy's balding head and speckled face filled the file labelled 'hatred' in his mind!

Anger welled and flooded his heart. *The Cat* raised its head, tilted it to one side. The cigarette smoke rose from Rick like he was a human chimney.

Natasha will never feel the sun on her skin again.

But Jimmy will! Oh yes you can bet that bunny has been burning his bald head all summer!

The Cat's tail flicked behind its head, it was nothing but a glaring shadow to Rick, the sun behind it, too bright.

Rick, the cigarette in his mouth, tilted his head to mimic *The Cat*, whose reflection stood out in the mirrored shades. It was his turn to stare.

What do you say, Buddy? Shall we invite good old Jimmy around for tea?

The Cat purred its agreement!

THE END

The Last Cast Of The Fly

1988 MELVOIR WATER:

The water was raging with white seahorses. The bow of the boat lurched forward, dropping then rising. Greg knew enough to know that he had to face this storm head on. Face this tempest.

He sat with freezing fingers, the colour of blue, gripping the throttle of the small, twelve-foot fishing boat. The engine groaned in angst against the task required of it. This was not just some mild downpour, as the weather forecast had predicted. This was the real thing.

Cold water spayed at Greg's face, shards of ice-cold needles on his skin. He grimaced. Karl sat in the bottom of the boat, the chain of the anchor that had been pulled up hastily was dangerously wrapped about his leg. Greg noticed this and considered shouting out against the wind and the hectic noise that surrounded them. He thought better of it.

Karl was not likely to move until they reached the wooden platform of safety that awaited them at the water's edge. Karl didn't like being on a boat at the best of times, let alone when it decided to turn into Shit City.

The fog was low and the visibility was almost zero. He didn't like to admit it to himself but he really was worried. He knew from experience that the water below reached depths of sixty foot. He had caught many a decent fish here in the past, including the nine-pound rainbow that had made Karl nearly choke himself on his own envy.

Greg could only guess the direction to face the boat. The dropping of the wooden frame and then the way that it rose back into the air, made him think rather sickly of the pirate ship ride he would refuse to go on when he was a kid.

He couldn't see the land. He knew it was about twenty minutes' full-throttle drive away from where they had anchored up. But he couldn't see it, this was Shit City alright.

Karl had a tight hold oh his hood with one hand, pulling it as far down as he could, a futile attempt to shield from the ice needles that peppered them like machine gunfire. He would turn his head as if to look at Greg, but he gave up after he realised the fog had encroached so much that he could hardly see the man steering his destiny, the man with whom he all-of-a-sudden entrusted his life.

Funny how quickly things can change, one minute you're casting a wet fly from a twelve-foot boat with your work buddy, the next you're huddled in the bottom of the boat preying that your buddy knows what the hell he is doing. They both knew this was bad. This could be damn near close to the wall.

As the engine droned and Greg tried with all his effort to ignore the quick glances of his friend, as he tried to make headway and not make any bad decisions, he had something else pecking away at his mind.

The man sat in front of him, the one with that Shit!-I'm-so-bloody-scared look slapped all over his face, was sleeping with his wife.

And that's what was really pecking away at Greg, like a woodpecker, TAT... TAT... TAT... TAT... on the back of his brain. It would soon make a hole there. His mind went back to the anchor chain wrapped about Karl's leg.

The needles peppered. And that woodpecker kept right on a pecking.

★ ★ ★

2018: SOMEWHERE IN CAMBRIDGESHIRE

Greg Rose carefully placed his old and dust-ridden Montana Fly reel into its waiting travel bag. There was a quiet love in his touch, the metal reminding him rather sombrely of better times. Not for more years than he dare think, had that reel been put to use.

Could it really be that long, has it been ten years? It can't be!

The truth was that it had actually been closer to fifteen years since Greg had been fishing, also he was well aware of this, but like a lot of retired gents, it didn't do to dwell on such things.

Time sure does fly.

With a quick snap of the old struggling zip, the leather bag concealed the reel. He grabbed the long scabbard tube containing his fly rod, snatched up his net and pole and was in his S-Type Jag. Three-litre engine powering its way towards the town of his birth.

Greg pulled into the gravel car park, his tyres spitting stones aside in his desire to rekindle the old flame he so yearned to reignite. The casting of the artificial fly, the age-old attempt tried by so many, to tempt the king of sports fish to take the hook.

He walked briskly over to the bailiff's cabin, reel bag and net pole slung over his aging shoulder. He moved with the vigour of a man twenty years his junior.

He paid for his ticket, received a quick overhaul on the water's rules and procedures, and with a rather overly warm 'thank you', he was standing on the wooden jetty, along which were moored over 20 twelve-foot fishing boats. The usual type found on reservoirs all over the country. They looked ominous to Greg, like a line of wild horses tethered and waiting to disappear with whoever dare approach them.

Greg stood still, his lonely figure cut out into the foreground of the picturesque scene. He stood as though he were a child, standing ready for his first day at school. Unsure, afraid.

He was alone on the wooden platform. The sound of the lake's water gently lapping against the panels was the only sound. Stillness, fiercely intense, draped about his surroundings. He felt a chill, a nervousness encroaching about him.

The smell of the water was flooding him. Prickling fears of unknown dangers, riddled with anxiety, invaded his otherwise calm and controlled mind.

It had been a long time since Gregory had been to Melvoir Reservoir. A long time indeed.

Scanning with slowly worsening eyes that had, in the past few years, required spectacles, he realised, with more than a little sickness to his stomach, just how little the place had changed. He could have sworn that the jetty, the wood dark-grey and creaking with the movement of the lake's lapping was, in fact, the very same as he remembered it to have been. The boats, although older, he was sure had also not changed, just faded paint proof of the passing of time.

Glancing down at the cracked and hardening skin of his own arms, Greg chuckled slightly in the March breeze.

The boats are not the only ones with the changes of time. That's for sure.

Two men came now, young men, the sight of them gave pull on the strings of his heart. There was no cracked or hardening skin there. They carried all manner of tackle, things that Greg had never seen before. They chatted intently together; they seemed to have so much to say to one another. They were totally unaware of the lonely old man not thirty yards from them, standing on the furthest point of the jetty. They scurried into a boat, the sudden charge of the petrol engine raking its way through the silence. A large stone dropped into still water. And they were gone, out of sight into the mist of the early spring morning.

Greg swallowed hard as he watched the little boat become nothing in the fog over the water's rippling surface. He remembered how it had been not that different the last time he had fished the water. How the weather had changed without warning, how the fog, rain and wind had galloped into his life.

His left arm began to ache.

Stop that! Don't think about that!

A deep throbbing ache as though he had caught his forearm in a vice. Dropping the reel bag, he clutched at the bony arm with wrinkled fingers of his right hand. Breathing deeply and swearing under his breath.

Bugger! Not now! Not now!

Angina! He had been diagnosed with the life-changing condition four years previously. He had been at work, highly paid and highly respected. Collapsing with server chest pain. The doctors had said that it was not a heart attack. That had been the one thing Greg had clung to.! Not a heart attack.

But a warning, none the less.

Two other men made their way along the groaning jetty. These were older men. Greg remarked to himself that they were not far from his own age.

"Morning, are you ok? Are you alone?"

The man who asked the question had genuine concern in his eyes, the kind that spoke not of sympathy but empathy. The water lapped at the wood.

Perhaps he has the same, perhaps he had a lying cheating wife, perhaps he had spent years, a lifetime, unsure, not knowing, seeing the light through the layers of deceit. Not even knowing if his kids... stop now! Your arm, stop now!

"I'm fine thank you, not a bad day for it; let's hope that the fish are on the feed!"

The response was a polite one. But the look didn't seem to leave those concerned eyes. It was possible that the man knew there were hidden depths in the polite answer of this strange old man. After passing pleasantries the second boat's engine roared and disappeared into the mist.

The pain in Greg's arm subsided; he subtly inhaled through his life-saver that he kept on him at all times. Not a heart attack, but a warning. Sharp bolts of oxygen hammered at his temples, but the pain passed.

Slowly and with tentative legs he lowered himself into the boat. Started the engine without difficulty and set himself to the task of remembering where he used to catch fish on the large water.

Now then. Let's have smoked trout for tea.

It had crossed Greg's mind more than once that the years that had separated him from fishing might have affected his ability.

Not at all!

He was anchored up, in a spot he knew to be quite deep, about sixty foot, if he remembered rightly. His fly line was dancing with perfect form through the air.

Ha Ha! Still got it!

He was very pleased with himself. The fog had partially lifted, letting great staves of sunlight strike though the passing clouds. The last time he had fished it had been under rather different surroundings. He and Wendy had travelled to Cuba, she for the fine weather and the beach, he for the chance to fish.

They had enjoyed their time together, he reminisced with quiet solitude, and warm weather had brought them closer than they had been in years, the clear blue of the water when they took out a boat. They had known it to be the last real holiday, the last before old age really clamped on the shackles. It had been her last holiday in any case, their last real time together. Wendy had died not long after getting back.

Plus, he couldn't be sure, then he never could, but he thinks she had been completely faithful the whole time.

Couldn't be sure. But he hoped so.

He was forced from this meandering of time, when his fly rod lurched violently forward, tugging and jumping in his hands; the bright yellow fly line pulled tight! He had a fish on. Lips parted in a cracking-teeth, winning smile, he giggled as the Rainbow jumped and dived giving him the most fun he had had in years. Finally he had it beaten.

Standing, legs apart to steady himself in the rocking boat, holding the fish in his hands. Blood ran from its gills in a steady trickle, finding his arm, the slime covered his fingertips.

His smile became a true winner, executive style. It was the biggest Rainbow Trout Gregory had ever had on his line, it was also his last.

There came a sudden jolt of the boat! Strong enough for him to drop the fish and fall into his wooden seat.

What the hell?

Greg, unsure and alarmed, still sitting on the wooden plank that made for the middle seat of the boat, grasped the metal rollicks on the port side. It had felt as though something had hit the boat from underneath. Absurdly the Loch Ness monster swam into his mind.

All went quiet. In fact the silence was screaming all around him. It happened again. A quick jerk, the boat rocking like a paper boat in the wild seas. Greg felt sure that water would soon pour over the boat's wooden edge. Waves billowed out from the boat's small frame.

His cold, wet fingers gripped harder at the rollicks, his mind numb with blind panic and shock.

The twelve-foot boat jerked once again. Pain began to grow in his arm and chest, he rummaged frantically for the life-saver in his pocket.

The boat jerked again, sending the little plastic inhaler flying out of his hand and into the water. Greg watched as it sank. Eyes brimming with tears, the inhaler had been more than just a medicinal help. It had been his comforter. A child with a blanket. Now it was gone.

The boat gave another fierce jolt, this time however Greg noticed something. The anchor chain, black and heavy, that hung over the starboard side, seemed to move with the jerking of the boat! He sat still, gripping the rollicks with increasing vigour.

The boat jerked. The chain rattled.

Greg, keeping himself seated on the wooden plank of a seat, slid himself across to the starboard side, finger wrapped around the circular wooden frame that made for the boat's edge. He found courage from deep within, he leant his head forward over the side. The black interlocking metal of the anchor chain crept deep down into the watery depths. Weed and scum that had drifted with the undercurrents snagged in the crevices.

The water, clearer now with the lifting of the fog and the brightness of the sun, Greg's eyes widened and his mouth opened wide. There, now only feet under the clear water's surface, was a face looking back up at him!

A face that was climbing the anchor's chain! A smiling face!

Greg threw himself into the bottom of the boat, hitting the back of his head on the engine's throttle. Too shocked even to make a sound, he just froze still. Fear's fingers tickled his sanity.

Two hands grasped the wooden rim of the boat, spitting out cold water onto Greg's face. The boat gave one last jerk as the body of a man, dressed in old fishing gear, lifted himself into the boat with ease, water dripping from him. His head was covered by a green hood. Greg could do nothing but lay there, in the bottom of the boat staring at the unnatural act that had jumped into his morning.

Terror stole its way into his sick heart.

The man, the new member of the crew, sat on the seat in the front of the boat. Removed his hood and continued to smile. Gregory Rose finally did something. He began to scream in a way he never thought it possible for a man to scream.

"Oh stop that, will you, for crying out loud! And give us a fag will you."

It was Karl's face. It was Karl's voice.

Christ! It's Karl. It's really him! But that can't be because… because…

"Because Karl is dead! Is that what you're thinking, Greg old chap? Well I won't disappoint you if you're worried. Karl's dead alright. Now give us a fag."

It was Karl's voice, just how it was thirty years ago! He was there right in front of Greg. Sat there like he used to. Knees together, hands placed either side of him, gripping the boat's edge. Shoulders hunched up, face smiling. His hair was so thick and black. Blue eyes sparkled in the sunlight. Teeth perfectly formed shouting out at him from behind the parted lips.

This is… This is not happening! This can't be happening. It just it can't be happening. You're… you're…

"Dead!"

He shouted the last word with a quavering voice, the chords that made the sound might well have been frayed beyond repair with the weakness they created.

"Greg. Give us a fag will you. There is a good chap. Don't go making a scene."

Greg stood up, new determination had gripped at him. This was just not possible. He knew that, he was imagining it. It was in his head. He had fallen when the boat had jerked, banging his head.

Yes that's it you banged your head, didn't you, on the throttle of the engine. That is it, you banged your head.

He rubbed at the sore spot he felt on the back of his head, feeling the bump and the thin wavering whips of white hair that sat there.

He stood, feet apart, hands now shot out in front of him towards the man sat there, like a goalkeeper poised for a penalty.

"Greg, old chap, you look ridicules. Now look, you can either sit down and hear what I have to say. Or you can just stand there looking like a well-past-it man on the brink of going completely crazy. The decision is yours. I have nothing pressing!"

Greg found himself sitting down, legs trembling; the motor's throttle that had hit him on his first fright, he now grasped with both hands. His new best friend, the throttle of a twelve-foot boat.

"And Greg, a fag if you don't mind! I think that you owe me that much, don't you."

With that Karl had leant forward, his smile more of a leering grin, the sort you might expect from a man passing regretful news to an enemy.

Greg fumbled in his top pocket, finding the pre-rolled cigarettes he kept for when he caught a fish. Despite all the insanity that was going on before him, he felt a twang of regret, there was only one, and he had rather been looking forward to it.

Karl took it, placed it between those perfect teeth, and with a quick flick of his thumb, there jumped a large green flame, the darkest green, rising from the top of his thumb nail. He lit the smoke, and inhaled the residue. Exhaling with that satisfied sound all smokers make when they have endured time without their vice.

"That's better. Thirty years is a long time for a smoker to have no smoke. Believe me."

Greg said nothing. He was sure this hallucination would soon pass, and he would find himself lying at the bottom of the boat, with a painful head.

He watched as Karl enjoyed smoking the roll up. The smoke, the sound of the water, the feel of the throttle in his grasp. It all seemed so real!

It's all so very real. How can this be? I must have banged my head something terrible.

"Oh it's real alright, Greg my old chap. You can bet your right leg on that."

With that, Greg noticed that the fishing trousers on Karl's right leg were badly torn and ripped, it seemed that there were some dark red stains on the skin.

"Now then. Greg old chap. Is that all you can say to me? It's been thirty years after all. Can you believe that.

Karl's voice had risen to an almost cry of disbelief.

"Thirty bloody years! Well, tell me. Come on Greg, I'm dying to hear. What have you been up to."

There was a writhing, wriggling menace in the words that had been almost spat out of Karl's mouth, which had taken on a rather less attractive look.

There had crept about the gums of his, what seemed now to be yellow teeth, a black residue. His eyes that had sparked blue, had, it seemed, taken on a tinge of black. A shark's eyes.

Silence. The cigarette still burned between the yellow skin of Karl's right fingers.

"Come now, Greg, don't be shy. You know me, don't you. After all this time, there must be so much that you could tell me. What have you been doing, do you still work at Baker Works? Are you running the show yet? Oh, I bet you're retired now, aren't you? Of course, silly me, you must be! I must apologise but you know it's rather difficult to keep track of time when you're sixty feet at the bottom a lake. Bet you can imagine, well enough. Hey Greg, old chap! Thirty years, it's a hell of a long time! Gets you thinking."

Greg coughed, a hard cough, his head was like a flannel wringing wet with shear confusion, this was not happening to him! He knew that he just had to wait, wait for the passing of time. And someone would find him, he had fallen and hit his head on the throttle. Someone would soon find him.

That's it. Just wait, let this image do its thing. I can wait. Just sit tight and you will soon wake up! Soon wake up!

"Oh, I'm sorry Greg, did I bore you with my ramblings. It's just been so long since I spoke to a living man. There's plenty of dead ones down there.

With that, Karl with cigarette held between index and middle finger, pointed over the side towards the water.

"But it's not the same you know. To speak to someone who has something new to say. There's only so much, 'I don't deserve this' and 'Why haven't they found me? I have a wife and kids' that you can listen to before it all gets a little repetitive. You understand me, don't you Greg old chap you understand what I'm saying, don't you?"

Greg, to his astonishment found himself nodding his head. He was listening, he was actually mesmerised by the vision before him. This was too much for him. He wanted the waiting to be over; he wanted to be back home. Back home with a glass of port in his hand.

"Good, I'm glad, I really would hate for you to be just pretending, that would not do at all, old chap."

Greg watched as Karl took another long drag on the cigarette. The fingers that held it had gone from being a yellow, to a dirty, dark, burnt colour, the thick black hair had thinned immensely, leaving pathetic wisps of grey mottled hair hanging dankly at Karl's shoulders.

"As you can probably see, we don't have long! I have some questions for you. You have no choice. You have to answer! Do you understand?"

"Yes, I understand." The thin, shredded vocal chords sounded as though they were on their last thread now.

"Have you enjoyed your life, Greg?"

"What?"

"It's quite simple!" Karl was shouting again. His blackened gums had become rotten with only a few stumps of ground teeth protruding from them, the clothes he was wearing had almost completely rotted away. They emanated a strong and distasteful stench in the air. Karl was rotting before Greg's eyes. Thirty years of decomposition, in a matter in minutes.

"Did you enjoy your life?"

Greg actually thought about this. Rather like the guilty party that secretly enjoys being questioned when caught.

Had he enjoyed his life? The answer was no! He knew that.

"It's been a full life. I don't know what you want me to say?"

The chords were finding more vigour now, strumming like a guitar, he was sure this would all be over soon. Besides he had nothing to hide.

"Greg, you have a heart with darker depths than any part of this bloody lake. And I would know. I've travelled every inch of the blasted place. There are fish, Greg. Such fish the likes of which you would never have dreamed of. They hide, Greg, they hide in the deepest places, hidden from the light. They stay where it is dark and lonely. Like you, Greg. Like you!"

Karl's face had lost any fat or shape, the hollow of his eyes had sunk low, the shark's eyes had become black holes that Greg had to turn away from.

"Don't you turn you back on me! Don't you dare!"

The scream vibrated across the air, shaking Greg, removing any strength he had gained; he shrunk down into a ball, his limbs shook once again, and all thought of escape, of leaving this terror had left him.

God! Good God! It's real. He is here, he is right here. His bloody face is falling off right in front of me. God help me, God help me, he is really here.

The rotting, stinking skin-peeling face of Karl grimaced, the rotten skull had maggots crawling between his jaw bones, worms wriggled about his leg bones, the was an indentation of chain etched into his right shin bone! Karl's rotten corpse pointed to this dead tattoo.

"There! You see that! Do you see that you bastard! Do you see how hard I tried, how hard I tried against water and steel, how I struggled to free myself, how my soul tore from me as I pulled and pulled as the skin and bone broke away! Do you see, do you see it, you bastard!"

Bits of flaking skin and dead maggots shook from the shaking corpse, the swollen, rotten tongue dangled from the black gums.

Greg shouted, his mind racing with regrets that he couldn't have explained in a thousand years.

"It was an accident! It was an accident. Damn it, Karl, I'm sorry, it was an accident. I tried. I tried, but I couldn't see, I couldn't see anything. The wind, the rain, the waves, it was too much I couldn't see. I didn't know the anchor chain was wrapped around your leg, I didn't know, it was just an accident, a terrible accident! If I could have saved you, I would have. The chain, it came loose. I'm sorry it came loose from the buckle. It wasn't my fault!"

"Liar! Filthy liar!"

The corpse stood now on feet whose nails had grown long and gnarled into bunches about the toes. The head was completely bald now. Patches of yellow skin fluttered in the air. Dust, flakes of dust on the water's surface. Just another day on the water.

"It's the truth. I cried. I cried for you… we both did."

There he said it. He had practically admitted to it.

There followed a silence. There was only black and ashen skin now on the face of the dead fisherman. Even so, it was smiling, a smile of the damned.

Gregory Rose hung his head and cried.

I'm so sorry. It just happened. I knew. I found your letters to her. I found them. The miserable letters. I found them. But you were saved. I saved you, she never changed. You were one of many. My children. The children I raised. Karl. Oh Karl, they are not mine. She never changed. I just did it. I didn't want to, it just happened. I cried, Karl. Oh, if you only knew how I cried. I cried so hard I thought I would die from it. I cried for you and for what I did!

Greg lifted his head, gasping air through old lungs. For the first time since the corpse had found its way into his life, he once again noticed the pain, the raging uncontrollable pain in his chest and left arm.

Karl's dead face was inches from his own. The maggots crept about the now-skinless skull that leered at him. There were dark eyes set deep within; the smell threatened to make him vomit.

The teeth parted.

"You're coming with me, Greg old chap. We all cry down there. Oh, you won't believe how we cry. You'll fit right in."

A dry, bony arm flung itself around Greg's neck. Lifting him to his feet. The corpse held him from behind. Greg could smell its breath. Dead breath. It held him by the neck. Greg pawed at the bones, his fingernails created a squeal on the hard surface.

God, no. I can smell the death on it! Please God, save me. Please, please!"

A large worm made its way out of the corpse's eye socket, poking its way into Greg's ear.

Gregory Rose shouted with all his might. The chords no longer frayed, he sounded like a young man, thirty again, afraid of bad weather and his wife's infidelity.

"Please! Karl, please, you don't know how I suffered. I saved you from her! Please Karl. No, I am sorry. I am sorry Pleeeasee!"

The corpse, breathing death onto the back of Greg's neck, whispered with coarse hatred.

"Suffered, Greg have you? Well, come with me! We all cry down here! We all cry! You can cry for me and I for you. We all of us cry, Greg."

With that, the corpse pulled Mr Gregory Rose under the water's surface. The ripples didn't settle for quite some time.

★ ★ ★

James Richards, Melvoir Waters' bailiff found the empty boat of Greg Rose when it failed to return at dusk; he used a mounted, high-powered torch to search the boat's interior. After returning to the cabin, he made the required calls. The police would arrive in half an hour, to take a statement.

It was an inconvenience, but one he had had to deal with before. It was the same old story. An old boy out on his own. Probably find out he had some medical condition that meant he shouldn't have been on the water in the first place! But nothing stopped these old foreman types.

Sure was funny though!

Mr Richards was not an easily spooked man. But it had seemed to him, from the very start, when the old boy had walked into the cabin that morning, it had seemed that he was set for something bad.

He just couldn't explain it. It had just crept along his spine after the old man had left, to find the boat. There had been something strange in his manner, the way he had shook his hand for too long, not letting him drop it when he felt time was enough. The way he had thanked him, a little too emphatically. It had seemed almost as though, well almost as though...

As though he was saying good-bye!

James Richards placed the glass of whisky on the desk in front of him. He would wait here for the police. He would say nothing of his fears. He would say nothing of the way the old man had given him the shivers, he would say nothing of the way that he had made him feel that tingle, the same tingle he sometimes got when he took the boat out at night on his own, the tingle that he got when he had found the empty boat, the same tingle he always got when he found an empty boat that had been occupied the day it was found.

He sipped the whisky. He would say nothing about the young man that had followed the old boy out of the cabin that very morning. The young man that was dressed in old fishing gear, the young man who had appeared from nowhere, who had looked at the old boy with intent. The young man who had cast a glance back at him before he had followed the old boy out, the young man who had smiled at him with black gums, the young man who had tears falling from his eyes.

Nope. Just another one of those old fisherman's tales.

James Richards drank his whisky and waited for the police. He had done this before, after all. Was just another day on the water of The Weepings' premier trout lake.

THE END